CASTAWAY

After his ship crashed, Nils Kruger had spent weeks wandering across the face of the planet . . . suffering from the blistering heat, the searing cold of an alien climate. Now he had found a fellow wanderer. And it was not human.

Nils had no way of knowing how helpess or how dangerous the alien might be, but it did look harmless.

Through months Nils and the creature marched together, shared adventure and escape—and grew to know each other. Then Nils made a disturbing discovery.

This creature, this thing called Dar, possessed a mind more powerful than his own . . . a mind totally retentive of facts, capable of interpretation and analysis— and with feelings and needs fully as strong as Nils's own.

And to this mind, Nils Kruger was the alien.

Books by Hal Clement

CYCLE OF FIRE
CLOSE TO CRITICAL
NATIVES OF SPACE

Available in Ballantine Books Editions

CYCLE OF FIRE

by

Hal Clement

BALLANTINE BOOKS . NEW YORK

SBN 345-01948-2-075

Library of Congress Catalog Card No. 57-9139

First Printing: April, 1957
Second Printing: January, 1959
Third Printing: June, 1970

Cover art by Dean Ellis

Printed in the United States of America

BALLANTINE BOOKS, INC.
101 Fifth Avenue, New York, N.Y. 10003
An Intext Publisher

I. LOGISTICS

CONSIDERING THE general nature of a lava field the glider had no business looking as sound as it did. Its tail assembly was intact; its fuselage had suffered only the removal of fabric from the lower side; even the narrow wings appeared undamaged. Had there been a catapult within three thousand miles one would have been tempted to try launching the craft. Even Dar Lang Ahn might have been deceived, if his eyes had been his only source of information.

He had more than eyes, however. He had been the unfortunate who had ridden the machine in. He had seen the pitted black surface of the flow suddenly sweep toward him as an unexpected wind had dragged him toward the nameless volcano; he had felt the impact and the partial rebound as the springy wood frame of the aircraft had done its best to absorb the shock; and, most important, he had heard both main wing spars fail. The first question in his mind was not how to get aloft again but whether or not he should wreck the glider more obviously before he left it, and that was not really a question. The real problem was raised by the books.

There were not many of these, of course; Ree Pell Un had been far too foresighted to trust a very large fraction of the city's knowledge to one aircraft. Still, they could not be ignored; it was his duty to get them intact to the Ice Ramparts, and eight hundred years is quite long enough to develop a strong devotion to duty. Dar Lang Ahn had lived that long.

Fortunately they were not heavy. He set resolutely to work making as much as possible into a pack that could be carried without hampering either his walking or his use of weapons. When he finally straightened up and started purposefully away from the wreck he was laden with perhaps half his own weight in books, a tenth as much food, and the crossbow and bolts which had been his inseparable companions since early life. The greater part of his food remained behind, but no reading matter.

He had thought about the direction to take while loading up. A great circle course to his intended destination was a shade over two thousand miles, of which roughly half was ocean. The way he had planned to fly was much longer, because of the islands which made it possible to get across that ocean in stages never greater than fifty miles. He decided to stick to this route, because he had already traveled it several times and knew the way. To be sure, the landmarks would look different from the ground, but that should not prove a great difficulty to his photographic memory.

He did not, of course, start in the direction he intended to maintain. That would have led almost directly over the mountain on whose flanks he had crashed. Dar was a better mountain climber than any human being ever would be, owing to natural advantages of physique, but the top of this mountain was emitting a faint, steady plume of yellow smoke, and the lava under his feet was, it seemed to him, rather warmer than sunlight could account for. Therefore, while his immediate goal on the near shore of the ocean lay to the northeast and the nearest edge of the lava straight north, he turned until the crimson sun he called Theer was to his left and behind him and the smaller, blue Arren straight behind, and started into the northwest.

A lava field is not easy to cross on foot, even without a heavy load. Laden as Dar Lang Ahn was, it is torture. His feet were tough enough to resist the sharp bits of rock which he could not avoid, but there was no such thing as a level path. Again and again he had to revise his estimate of the time the journey would take, but he never admitted to himself that he might not complete it.

2

Twice he ate and drank, if the token sip and nibble that he took could be called by such names. Both times he kept walking. There were less than fifty miles between the place where the glider had crashed and the edge of the lava sheet, but if he were to fall asleep before crossing those miles he would almost certainly die of thirst. There was no water on the lava, so far as he knew, and with summer approaching he needed water as badly as a human being would in the same situation.

The first of his meals found him far enough from the mountain to turn northward, putting Theer directly behind him. Arren was catching up with the red sun, but shadows were still short. Accustomed though he was to two light sources, the presence of both suns made it a little more difficult to judge the terrain more than a few dozen yards ahead, and consequently he frequently missed short cuts.

Still, he made progress. The second "meal" found him out of sight of the volcano and a few hours later he was sure he could see a line of green ahead. This might, of course, have been a mirage, with which Dar Lang Ahn was totally unfamiliar. It might also have been a denser covering of the spiky, pulpy, barrel-shaped plants which grew here and there on the lava itself. The traveler, however, felt sure that it was real forest—plants whose presence would mean a plentiful supply of the water he was beginning to want badly. He gave the equivalent of a grin of relief, resettled the pack of books across his shoulders, drank off the rest of his water, and started once more for the horizon. He discovered his mistake some time before he actually became thirsty again.

Traveling in anything like a straight line he could have walked the distance to the forest easily. Even with the sort of detours he had been forced to make on the lava field he could cover it before suffering too seriously from thirst. He simply had not counted on extraordinary detours, since he did not remember seeing from the air anything different from the general run of cracks and ridges on the lava flow. His memory did not betray him, as it turned out, but the terrain did.

Theer had nearly ceased his westward travel and was rising noticeably, preparing for his yearly swoop back toward Arren, when Dar Lang Ahn found the barrier. It was not a wall, which he would never have considered impassable in any case; it was a crack—a crack which must have formed after the lava mass as a whole had almost completely hardened, for it was far too deep and long to have been caused by the mere splitting of a bit of hardened crust under the pressure of fluid from below.

He had never noticed it from above simply because it was not straight; it snaked its way among the more ordinary irregularities of the region, so that he had traveled along it for more than an hour before he grasped the actual situation. That was when the crack began to curve back toward the now distant volcano.

When he did realize what was happening Dar Lang Ahn stopped instantly and sought the shade of an upjutting slab of rock before he even began to think. He did not pause to berate his own foolishness, though he recognized it clearly enough; he concentrated on the problem that faced him.

The walls of the crevasse were unclimbable. Normally lava hardens in a surface rough enough to permit the claws of one of his people to get a grip on a nearly vertical surface, but this had been a split through the whole mass. True, the rock was full of gas bubbles and many of these had been opened by the crack and were large enough to furnish him support, but these occurred only near the surface. The opposite wall of the crevasse showed that only a few yards down the bubbles shrank to pinpoint size and, for practical purposes, vanished. Besides, the wall was not merely vertical. It "waved" so that no matter where he started down—or from which side, had he had a choice—he would find an overhang before descending very far. No, climbing was out.

4

The gap was too wide to jump—in most places too wide even for one without a burden, and Dar Lang Ahn never thought of abandoning his load.

He had no rope and not enough harness on his body or pack to improvise a line that would reach even as far as he could jump. Nothing grew on the lava from which either a rope or a bridge could be fashioned. The plants proved to be of a pulpy texture inside, quite without woody tissue, and the skins were not even tough enough to resist his claws.

The thing that delayed him longest in finding a solution was, of course, his determination not to be separated from the books. It took him an unbelievably long time to get the idea that the separation need not be permanent; he could throw the books across the gap and then jump himself.

This disposed of nearly all the difficulties, since he recalled several places where he was pretty sure of being able to jump across the crack if he was unhampered. He simply had to find one where a reasonably flat area existed, within reach of his throwing arm, on the far side of the crevasse.

He found it eventually. For the moment he did not think of the hours that had passed; he simply slid his pack to the black surface, checked to make sure that it was securely fastened—he wanted no risk of books falling out as it flew—tested its weight calculatingly with one powerful arm, and then, swinging around completely after the manner of a hammer thrower, launched it across the crack. There never was any doubt that it would get there; actually it went a little farther than Dar Lang Ahn had hoped and for an instant he wondered whether it might not reach the rough ground just beyond his target area. It finally stopped rolling, however, in full view and apparently intact, and with that assurance he planned his leap and made it.

He would have given no more details than that, had he been preparing a report of the incident. Most men

5

would have had difficulty in avoiding mention of their feelings as they rushed toward the edge, put every bit of effort they could raise into a leap as they reached it, looked for an instant into the sickening depth below, and then thudded painfully into rough, sharp, hard lava on the other side. One man did have a good deal to say about it, later. Dar Lang Ahn felt all the appropriate emotions as he went through this series of actions, but with the leap behind him he thought only of the books. He went on.

Theer was visibly higher when he encountered another crevasse between himself and the forest. This took less time to cross but still contributed its bit of delay; and finally, with the red sun well above the horizon and seemingly twice as large as it had appeared from the site of the glider crash, he was forced to admit to himself that he was going to be on the lava flow through the summer—and this was no time of year to spend a summer far from a large supply of water.

His death, then, would come somewhat earlier than he had expected, and something would have to be done about the books. Presumably there would be searchers when he failed to return home in a reasonable time, and he was close enough still to the usual air route between Kwarr and the Ice Ramparts for his location to be covered without the need for much imagination on any searcher's part. What was needed was something to make his position visible from the air. He considered trying to return to his glider but realized he could never make the journey—for one thing he would be too weak to get across the deep cracks by the time he reached them. Of course, if he had realized how small his chances of crossing the lava field actually were he would never have brought the books from the aircraft in the first place; it had simply never occurred to him to doubt his ability to make the trip. Now he had to rectify his error, or at least make it possible for someone else to do so.

He had left no visible trail on the rock, naturally, so

that finding his glider would do no good to the searchers. They would know the general direction that he had taken, of course, but since they would not know the precise time of the crash there would be no way for them to tell how far he might have traveled. They would not guess, any more than he had, that he might not have reached the edge of the lava flow; no one had any first-hand knowledge of the conditions so near a volcano.

His own body would not show against the lava to an observer at any likely altitude, for neither his size nor his coloring rendered him conspicuous. Since all the rocks were of nearly the same color he could not make any sort of contrasting pattern which could be seen from the air. There was nothing in his pack which would make a decent-sized signal flag or serve to paint anything on the rocks. The only things about him which held any possibility of use in this problem, as far as Dar Lang Ahn could see, were the buckles of his harness.

These were flat and of polished iron; they might serve as mirrors, though they were pretty small. Still, where there was no other hope he would have to make them do. He reached this decision while still plodding northward.

The question that remained was whether he should stop where he was and devote his remaining time to perfecting an arrangement of buckles which would have a maximum chance of catching a passing flier's eye, or keep on until he was obviously near the end. The latter alternative had the advantage of giving him a chance to reach some particularly advantageous spot—perhaps some spire of rock or configuration of lava slabs which would help catch a searcher's eye. That it also included a possibility of his finding water in time to save his own life was a point he did not consider; so far as he thought about that matter he was dead already. The only advantage of stopping now was that he could spend the rest of his life in the shade, which might be more comfortable than traveling farther under the blaze of the two suns. As might have been expected, he elected to continue walking.

He walked, or scrambled, or climbed, as circumstances required, while the red sun continued to rise and grow. It was starting to swing back in an eastward direction, too, but Arren's steady motion toward the west made him, at least, still useful as a guide. Perhaps Dar's course corrections were a little vague; perhaps his path, toward the end, could hardly be called a course at all, for as time passed and temperature mounted his mind dwelt more and more on the torturing thirst messages which his body was sending it. A human being would have been dead long since—dead and baked dry. However, Dar Lang Ahn had no perspiration glands, since his nerve tissue could stand temperatures almost as high as the boiling point of water, and in consequence he did not lose the precious liquid nearly as rapidly as a man would. A little went, however, with each breath that passed out of his lungs, and the breaths were becoming ever more painful. He was no longer sure whether the wavering of the landscape in front of him was due to heat or his own eyesight; frequently he had to turn both eyes on the same object to be sure he was seeing it accurately. Short spurs of rock seemed, for brief instants, to take on a semblance of living creatures; once he caught himself starting to leave his chosen path in order to investigate a slab of lava. It took long seconds for him to convince himself that nothing could really have dodged behind it. Nothing lived here; nothing *could* move. The sounds which reached his ears were simply the crackings as new patches of lava were caught by the sunlight and warmed. He had heard them before.

Still, it had been a very convincing motion. Perhaps he should go back to see——

Go back. That was the one thing he must not do. That, of all possible actions, was the one provably useless one. If illusions were snatching at his mind in such a way as to tempt him into an act like that he must have come closer to the end than he thought. It was time to settle

8

down and set up his reflector while he still had control of his muscles.

He wasted no time in regrets, but stopped where he was and looked around carefully. A few yards away a slab of hardened lava had been broken from the crust and tilted up almost perpendicularly by the pressure of liquid rock underneath. Its upper edge was a good ten feet above the surface in the immediate neighborhood. This was more than twice Dar Lang Ahn's height, but the sheet was rough enough to give a grip to his claws and he saw no reason to expect difficulty in setting up his buckles at the top.

He unslung the pack of books and lowered it to the hot rock. He made sure it was closed tightly and fastened it in position with one of the pack straps; it would probably rain even here when summer was over, and he could not afford to have the books spoiled or washed away.

Then he removed his harness and checked its individual straps with one eye, while he examined with the other the ridge where he planned to set the buckles. Two or three pieces of leather which seemed superfluous he laid beside the pack; the rest, with the buckles, he strapped once more about his body in order to leave both hands free for climbing.

The upper edge of the slab was as jagged as it had appeared from below and he had little difficulty in snagging the straps around the projections. He arranged one buckle so that its reflected beams pointed southward, rising at a small angle; the other he tried to set for the eyes of a searcher directly overhead. Neither, of course, was very likely to attract attention—they really depended only upon Arren's light, since the red sun would only be above the horizon for a short time before and after summer and the air lanes would be empty during the hot season itself. Still, it was the best that Dar Lang Ahn could do, and with the bits of metal arranged to his satisfaction he took one more look around before descending.

The landscape was shimmering more than ever. Once

again he felt almost sure that he had seen something disappear behind a slab of rock, in the direction from which he had come. He dismissed the illusion from his mind and began to climb down, paying close attention to his hand and foot holds; he had no wish to spend his remaining few hours with the agony of a broken bone, even if there was no way to make the time really comfortable.

He reached the bottom safely and, after a few moments' thought, dragged his book pack into the shadow of the ridge. Then he settled himself calmly, using the pack as a pillow, folded his arms across his chest, closed his eyes, and relaxed. There was nothing more to do; perhaps his centuries-trained sense of duty was not exactly satisfied, but even it could not find a specific task to make him perform.

It would be nearly impossible to put his thoughts into words. No doubt he regretted dying earlier than his fellows. Quite possibly he considered the bleak landscape spread before him and wondered idly just how much farther he would have had to get in order to live. However, Dar Lang Ahn was not human, and the pictures which formed most of his thoughts, being shaped by an eyesight and cultural background drastically different from those of any human being, could never be properly translated to the mind of a person of Earth. Even Nils Kruger, as adaptable a young man as might be found anywhere and who certainly became as well acquainted with Dar Lang Ahn as anyone could, refuses to guess at what went on in his mind between the time he settled down to die and the time Kruger caught up with him.

The boy's approach went unheard by Dar, keen though his ears normally were. He was not entirely unconscious, however, for the scent of water affected him enough not only to snap his eyes open but to send him bounding to his feet. For just an instant his eyes roved wildly about in all directions, then they both fastened on the figure toiling over the rock a dozen yards away.

Dar Lang Ahn had never before had reason to distrust

10

either his memory or his sanity, but this time he felt that something must be wrong with one or the other. This living thing was shaped correctly, more or less, but the size was unbelievable. It towered a good foot above his own four feet and a half, and that was simply *wrong*. The other oddities were minor—eyes in the front of its face, a beaklike projection above the mouth, pinkish coloration instead of purplish-black—but the height put it out of any class which Dar could drag from his memory. *People*, other than accident victims who had had to start over, were four and a half feet tall, just now; Teachers were a little under eight. There was nothing between those limits that walked on two legs.

Then even the size was driven from his thoughts by another fact. The smell of water that had roused him was coming from this creature; it must be literally drenched with the stuff. Dar Lang Ahn started to move toward the newcomer as this realization struck him, but he stopped after the first step. He was too weak. He groped backward, seeking support from the slab of rock in whose shadow he had been lying. With its aid he held up while the unbelievable thing approached; then, with the scent of water burning his nostrils, everything seemed to let go at once. A curtain dropped in front of his eyes and the rough stone at his back ceased to hurt. He felt his knees give, but not his impact with the lava.

II. DIPLOMACY

IT WAS the taste of water that roused him, as its scent had a few minutes before. For long moments he let the liquid trickle into his mouth without opening his eyes or noticing anything peculiar in its taste. He could feel the strength flow back into his body along with the precious fluid and he simply enjoyed the sensation without even trying to think.

That, of course, could not last after his eyes were open, and finally he did open them. What he saw was sufficient to bring his mind to full alertness almost instantly.

It was not that the human face so close to his was weird in appearance; that appearance had already been engraved on his memory before he collapsed and it caused him no surprise now. It took only a few seconds of consciousness to allow him to realize that this creature was not a *person* as he understood the term, but that it evidently was not unfriendly and not entirely lacking in good sense. It was providing the water which was reviving him, after all. The tension Dar Lang Ahn felt at this point was due not to surprise at Kruger's presence or appearance, therefore, but to astonishment at the source of water. The strange thing was actually squeezing into his open mouth one of the pulpy plants. This act gave rise to the first of the misunderstandings which were to complicate the friendship of the two for a long time to come.

Dar Lang Ahn concluded instantly that Kruger must be a native of the volcano region, since he had such surprising knowledge of its plant life. This, naturally, caused him to regard the boy with more than a little uneasiness. Kruger, on his part, had been following the native from the time of the glider crash, had seen him ignore consistently the plants which so closely resembled Earth's cacti, and had only with the greatest difficulty been able to persuade himself that the little being's obvious distress was caused by thirst.

Had their positions been reversed Kruger would, of course, have felt properly grateful to anyone or anything which had supplied him with water, whether it was human or a walking pineapple, but he knew perfectly well that "proper gratitude" was not a universal trait even with his own kind. Therefore the moment that Dar Lang Ahn's eyes opened the boy laid the partly squeezed cactus down within the native's reach and stepped backward. Personal caution was only part of his reason; he wanted to relieve any possible fear that the creature might feel.

Dar Lang Ahn handled immediate problems first. With one eye held on his strange helper—he did not know for a long time the uneasy sensation that very act could arouse in a human being—he used the other and one hand to find, pick up, and return to his mouth the plant whose juices had revived him. He kept it there for a long time, convinced that he would be able to use the last drop of fluid he could squeeze from it, but before it was quite empty another thought struck him. It made him pause.

Kruger saw the mangled plant leave his new acquaintance's mouth after what seemed a long time and found himself wondering a little tensely what would happen next. He was not really afraid, since the native was so much smaller than he, but he was experienced—or open-minded—enough to realize that size and potentiality for damage might not go quite hand in hand. He hoped, naturally, that some move would be made which he could interpret beyond doubt as a friendly one, but he could not, offhand, imagine what action could be so free of uncertainty. Dar Lang Ahn managed to find one, however.

With an effort that was obvious even to the human being and which nearly dropped the little messenger back into unconsciousness, he rose to his feet. Carefully, still keeping one eye on Kruger, he made his way out into the sunlight to a point some twenty yards from his protecting rock. Here he stopped for a moment and gathered strength, then bent over, wrenched another cactus free, sucked briefly at the oozing base to make sure it was the same sort as the one he had just used up, returned to the rock—and gave the plant to Kruger. The boy mentally took off his hat to a mind apparently quicker than his own, accepted the gift, and drank from it. Five minutes later the two were seated side by side trying to make sense out of each other's sounds.

Each party, of course, had a few mental reservations about this developing friendship. Dar Lang Ahn could not forget the suspicion naturally engendered by his companion's familiarity with lava-field vegetation; Kruger was trying to make fit together the other's apparent ignorance of those same plants and what appeared to be an equally evident intelligence. It occurred to him that Dar was no more a native of this world than he himself, but he had seen the crash of the glider and spent some time examining the aircraft after the pilot had left it. It seemed beyond the pale of possibility that a visitor from another world would be traveling in such a conveyance; either he would be in his ship, or some auxiliary of it, or on foot like Kruger himself. There was a possibility on this line, though, at that. Perhaps this little manlike thing was a castaway like Kruger but had shown more ingenuity than the boy and managed to build the glider himself. That tied in with the speed of thought he—or she or it—had already shown, though it made Nils a trifle uncomfortable.

Human beings have a strong tendency to cling to whatever hypothesis they may evolve to explain some new situation. Hence, while the suggestion that Dar Lang Ahn was a member of a race foreign to this world and quicker-witted than his own hurt his pride, the notion stayed in Kruger's mind—and grew, during the days that followed, to something like a certainty.

Dar had an advantage over his new acquaintance in this respect. His strongest prejudices were not those in favor of his own ideas but those the Teachers and their books had instilled into him. Neither had ever mentioned anything like Nils Kruger, so he was free to form idea after idea concerning the strange creature's nature. He liked none of them. Therefore, he continued to think, while the strength flowed back into his muscles.

One thing was evident: this creature was intelligent and presumably had some natural means of communication. So far it had not shown evidence of possessing a voice, but that could easily be checked. Tentatively, Dar Lang Ahn spoke a few words to the larger being.

Kruger answered at once, producing a series of perfectly meaningless noises as far as Dar was concerned but at least showing that he did possess a language. This was one of the few experiences shared by the two which left them with the same impression; on this occasion they decided simultaneously that language lessons were in order and settled down to conduct them. It was too hot to travel, anyway, and Dar still needed to get some strength back.

The shadow of the rock ledge was growing narrower as the two suns separated—the near-eclipse had occurred during Dar's wait for death—but it was still broad enough to shield both of them. Kruger settled down with his back against the ledge; Dar resumed his former position, using the pack for a pillow.

There are several ways to learn a language. Unfortunately, there was only one possible with the resources at hand and even for that the material was a trifle scanty. A lava field with an occasional cactus, a respectable number of shadows, and two suns shining on it furnishes demonstration material for very few nouns and practically no verbs. Plenty of adjectives may apply to it, but it is decidedly difficult to make clear just which one is being used at the moment.

Kruger thought of drawing pictures, but he had neither pencil nor paper and the sketches he made on the lava surface with a broken bit of rock didn't look like much even to their author when he had finished. They certainly meant nothing to Dar.

Nevertheless a few sounds gradually acquired more or less the same meaning to both parties. To describe their exchange of ideas as a conversation would be rank deception, but ideas did get across. By the time the red sun had disappeared below the southeastern horizon it was mutually understood that they would proceed together to the edge of the lava field to find something more drinkable than cactus juice and more edible than the rather nauseating pulp of the plants.

Kruger was not too happy about this, as a matter of fact. In the months he had been on the planet he had walked some three thousand miles northward to get away from the periodically intolerable heat of the red sun, and in the last few hundred had realized that he was see-ing progressively more of the blue one. The reason was obvious enough: the blue star was a "circumpolar" in the northern part of the northern hemisphere—or, as the *Alphard*'s navigator would have to put it, its declination seen from this planet was at least several degrees north. The trouble was that Kruger had not the faintest idea of the motion of the planet relative to the blue star; he could not even guess whether it would produce a notice-able seasonal effect or not and if it did, how long the sea-sons would last.

He had been toying with the idea of heading south-ward again for several weeks before he had seen Dar's glider in flight. That was the first intimation he had had, other than the rather doubtful cases of lights seen from space by the *Alphard*'s observers, that there were people of any sort on the planet; he had set out in the direction the glider had been taking. It was sheer luck that he had been close enough to see Dar's crash—or rather that the crash had occurred so close to the spot where Kruger had happened to be. He had followed the little pilot for several days; he had leaped the same crevasses as Dar had, taking an even deadlier risk with his greater weight and not-so-much-greater strength, but not daring to lose track of the being; and he had been shocked profoundly to discover his guide down and apparently helpless in the midst of the lava desert. He had hoped even then, somewhat illogically, that he could learn from the creature of some place to the south, out of the permanent glare of the blue sun, where he could find shelter and civilized company; after all, while the glider had been going north, it must have been coming from somewhere.

Still, if the pilot wanted to continue to the north there seemed nothing to do but string along. Presumably he was trying to reach a place where he would be comfortable; Kruger realized that he himself had no means of telling just what that would mean in terms of temperature, food, and water, but at least his companion did not enjoy the lava plain any better than a human being would. With that much in common the risk of staying with him seemed well worth taking.

It was a good deal cooler when the red sun finally set, and Kruger knew from past experience that it would be seven or eight earthly days before it rose again in this latitude. They were both hungry, but far from starving, and Dar Lang Ahn had recovered much of his strength in the sixty or seventy hours since Kruger's arrival. The blue star had moved around to the southwest, but it would be quite a number of earthly days yet before it would hamper their travel by shining in their faces.

They traveled more slowly than Dar had when he thought he was alone. The principal reason lay in Kruger's physical make-up; no human being can be as agile as the small, loose-jointed natives of Abyormen. Enough of the travel was climbing for Dar's clawed hands and feet to make a good deal of difference, and weak though the

17

native still was he had to hold back frequently for his bulkier companion.

Nevertheless they did make fair progress. No more major cracks were encountered, and after a few dozen hours of travel patches of soil began to appear here and there on the lava. Vegetation became thicker and from time to time pools of water stood in hollows in the lava. Evidently they were nearing the edge of the flow, since the lava itself was too porous to retain the liquid. The pools were scummed and crusted with rather smelly vegetation similar to the algae with which Kruger was familiar, and both travelers were willing to stick a little longer to cactus juice rather than drink from them; but their very presence improved morale. Dar hitched his pack of books a little higher and seemed to double his speed. The going became easier as more and more of the irregularities in the lava were filled with soil, though the soil itself was becoming more and more covered with vegetation. The plants at first were small in size, reminiscent to Kruger of lawn shrubs, but as the frequency of ponds increased and the amount of lava showing above the dirt grew smaller, the plants became larger, ranging finally to full-sized trees.

Most of these growths were as familiar to Kruger as to Dar, since the boy had seen them in profusion during his journey from the south; and he kept his eyes open for some whose stems or leaves he had learned were safe. He was in no mood to try any others; when Dar saw something he knew and offered it to his companion, Kruger shook his head.

"Nothing doing. Everything I've eaten on this world I had to try first, with no means of telling whether it would feed me or kill me. Out of five tries I got two bad bellyaches, and I'm lucky that was all. I'll wait until we see something I know, thanks."

Dar understood absolutely nothing of this except the refusal, which he filed in his mind as something else requiring explanation. He took as a working hypothesis the

18

idea that the boy knew and disliked the leaf in question; that supposition at least fitted in with the theory that Kruger was a native of the lava region.

By the time the blue sun had moved around to the west the trees were thick enough to shade them from it most of the time, and the undergrowth dense enough to impede them both quite seriously. Neither had any cutting tools except for a small sheath knife which had been part of Kruger's space-suit kit, and this was virtually useless for cutting a path.

The result was that they traveled very slowly. The impatience Dar felt did not show in his outward expression, at least to one as unfamiliar with his facial expression as Kruger was.

Language lessons continued as they traveled, with somewhat more speed because of the better supply of referents. Kruger felt that they should by now be getting ideas across to each other quite well and couldn't understand why this didn't seem to be happening. A lot of nouns were clear to both and a fair number of verbs. Adjectives, now that a great many articles were at hand for comparison, were increasing in supply. Once there are trees of various sizes the meaning of "big" and "little" can get across; if the attempt is made with a big rock and a small cactus there is no way to tell whether size, color, shape, or something entirely different from any of these is under discussion.

Nevertheless something was wrong. Kruger was gradually coming to suspect that his companion's language contained only irregular verbs and that each noun belonged to a different declension. Dar, for his part, more than suspected that Kruger's language was richer in homonyms than any useful tongue should be; the sound "tree," for example, seemed to mean a vegetable growth with long, feathery, purplish leaves, and another with a much shorter trunk and nearly round leaves, and still another which actually varied in size from one specimen to the next.

They did not dare let the language problems occupy their full attention. The jungle contained animal life and not all of it was harmless. Dar's sense of smell warned them of some flesh-eaters but by no means all; several times he had to resort to his crossbow while Kruger stood by holding his knife and hoping for the best. On one or two occasions animals apparently were frightened off by the alien human odor. Kruger wondered whether any of them would refuse to eat his flesh for similar reasons but felt no impulse to solve this problem experimentally.

In their first hundred hours in the jungle Dar killed a medium-sized creature which he proceeded to dissect with his companion's knife and eat with great glee. Kruger accepted a piece of the raw flesh with some inner doubts but decided to take a chance. It was against all the rules, of course, but if he had obeyed the rules about testing all food before eating it he would have starved some months before. In the present case the stuff was edible if not delicious and after eight or ten hours of waiting he decided that he had added another item to his limited list of permissible foods.

When they first entered the jungle Dar had changed their course to the northeast. Kruger had endeavored to find out why and, as their stock of useful words increased, finally got the idea that his companion was trying to reach either a lake or sea—at any rate a great deal of water seemed to be involved. This seemed desirable, although there was no longer a drinking problem owing to the numerous brooks they crossed. Kruger had already found out that rain could be expected quite regularly this far north for a hundred hours or so before and perhaps half as long after the rising of the red sun. Where he had started his journey, much farther south, this star was in the sky all the time while the blue one followed a rising and setting pattern of its own; there the weather was much less predictable.

The rain he was expecting had not arrived, however,

when he noticed that something seemed to have attracted Dar's attention. Kruger knew his companion could hear, though he was still unsure of the location of his ears, so he began to listen himself. At first nothing but the usual forest sounds were detectable—leaves and branches moving in the wind, the scurrying of thousands of tiny living things, the occasional drip of water from leaves, which never seemed to cease no matter how long a time had passed since it had rained—but Dar changed course a trifle; certainly he must hear something. They had gone another half-mile before it began to register on Kruger's ears.

When it finally did he stopped with an exclamation. Dar Lang Ahn swiveled one eye back toward him and stopped too. He knew as little of human facial expressions as Kruger knew of his, but even so he recognized the change of skin color that the sound produced in the boy's features.

"What?" Dar uttered the sound they had come to agree upon as a general interrogative.

"I think we'd better stay away from that."

"What?" It was a repetition of the former question, not the more specific interrogative which would have suggested understanding of Kruger's words.

"It sounds like . . ." The boy stopped; there were simply no available words. He fell back on signs. Unfortunately his first gesture was back in the direction from which they had come, and Dar took it to mean that Kruger had encountered this thing, whatever it was, before they had met. He was right but he did not grasp his companion's extreme reluctance to meet it again. After a few moments' silent regard of the boy's signals he gave it up and started on his way once more.

"Stop!" This was another word on which they had managed to agree, and Dar obeyed, wondering. They were far from the lava field; was it possible that this creature knew something about jungle that Dar himself didn't? The sound was strange to the native, of course;

that was why he wanted to investigate it. Was the giant actually afraid of it? If so, some thought was indicated. If whatever was making this sound could harm Kruger it was more than likely to be able to do as much to Dar. On the other hand perhaps it was merely a matter of dislike. In that case Dar would be passing up a chance for knowledge which might prove worthwhile material for a book. The question seemed to lie, then, between a risk of losing what books he had and one of failing to improve them. The risk of life involved meant nothing, of course, but both the other points were serious.

Perhaps he could get a better measure of the risk by seeing how far Kruger was prepared to go to keep them from this phenomenon. With this thought in mind Dar Lang Ahn deliberately turned once more and again started walking toward the irregular, dull, "Plop, plop, plop," that was now coming clearly through the trees.

Kruger was in a quandary. He had never dreamed of having to impress his opinions on Dar by force; he was not sure what the result of trying it would be. In any case he did not want to do anything that might give rise to enmity or even any more distrust than could be helped. In the circumstances he did the only thing that was left. Dar, rolling an eye back toward the human being, saw him start to follow and proceeded on his way assured that there was no real danger. He increased his speed, so far as the undergrowth rendered that possible. In a few minutes the vegetation cleared enough so that real walking could take the place of the laborious pushing aside of branches and vines. To Dar, this was a help; to Kruger, a confirmation of a fact that the increasing sound had already proved.

"Dar! Stop!" The native obeyed, wondering what had happened to change the situation; then he watched in surprise while Kruger forged past him and took up the lead. With his own equivalent of a shrug, he followed. The human being was going more slowly than he would have liked but perhaps there was a reason for it.

There was. In another hundred yards the undergrowth vanished, and at almost the same point the trees stopped. In front of them lay a bare, smooth-surfaced clearing nearly fifty yards across.

To Dar, this was simply a spot in which travel was easy; he would almost certainly have plunged on into the open, eager to get across and resume his journey toward the source of the mysterious sound. However, he was stopped. For the first time in their relationship Kruger not only touched him but blocked his path firmly with an arm more than strong enough to do the job. Dar looked at his companion in surprise, then his eyes traveled on about the clearing. His efforts to force his way past his big companion ceased and both eyes focused on the center of the open space.

The source of the sound was there. The clearing, for the most part, seemed to be floored with some smooth, hard material, but the center was in a constant state of motion—a great cauldron of liquid, sticky mud, heaving upward every few seconds to give birth to a great bubble which burst with the "plop" they had been hearing and released a cloud of vapor that drifted lazily away.

Kruger let his companion look for a minute or two; then, repeating his word to "Stop!" he went back on their trail a few paces. Rocks are not ordinarily easy to find on a jungle floor, but they were still close enough to the big flow for occasional outcrops of lava to be present. He found one of these, with a good deal of effort knocked off a fair-sized corner, brought it back, and tossed it out onto the apparently hard surface. The crust of dried mud gave, and the lava boulder vanished with a splash.

"I don't like these places," Kruger said firmly, indifferent to the fact that Dar could not understand him. "I went through one myself a few months ago and when I got out by working back up the tree root that had stopped my sinking—and incidentally knocked me out for quite a while—I found my name carved on the tree with several remarks about what a nice young fellow I'd been. I don't blame them for leaving me; they have every reason to suppose I'm still sinking. Living through it once, though, doesn't mean I'm going to try it again; my space suit is a long, long walk from here!"

Dar said nothing but promised himself to heed the advice of his friend as long as they were anywhere near the big fellow's native volcanic region. This was certainly something for the book!

III. PEDAGOGY

THE MUD GEYSER, and several others, had been left miles behind, but an occasional lava outcrop still kept Dar following Kruger's lead. The direction of travel was still to the northeast—the boy had made no attempt to change that—but in some subtle fashion the relationship between the two had changed.

For one thing the inevitable mistrust that they had felt at the beginning was just as inevitably fading. Another change, less logical in origin, was due to the almost comical misunderstanding which had resulted in Dar's firm conviction that Kruger was a native of the little-known volcanic areas of Abyormen, while Kruger himself was just as sure that Dar Lang Ahn did not belong on the planet at all. As a result Dar was constantly looking to Kruger for advice. If he shot a new type of animal—new, that is, to him—he would wait for the boy's verdict before eating it. Naturally quite a lot of perfectly good meat was wasted, since Kruger was in no hurry to risk his health and life testing new types of food.

At last, however, Dar killed a creature of the same type as the one the human being had tried when they first entered the jungle. The pilot did not even ask questions about this one; he borrowed the knife and set to work. Kruger looked at his portion with some distaste when it finally came.

He did not like raw meat, though it had certainly not harmed him the other time. On that occasion he had not suggested stopping to make a fire, since Dar was the moral leader of the association and his idea of a meal was apparently to eat on the spot whatever could not be carried and nibble at the rest as he went along. Now, however, with matters waiting on Kruger's advice and opinions, he chose to cook his meal.

He had salvaged all the material from his space suit which seemed likely to be of use and which was not too awkward to carry. While a fire-lighter is in no sense normal space-suit equipment, he had improvised one from the tiny sun-battery and a coil and condenser from the radio. He used it now, to the utter fascination of Dar Lang Ahn. Satisfied that its spark was still good he went looking for dry fuel.

This is not too common in a rain forest, but Kruger had had plenty of practice locating it before he had reached the lava field. Dar, utterly ignorant of what he wanted, simply followed and watched, munching his own share of the meat as he did so. He was interested in a detached sort of way, feeling that possibly whatever was going on might be worth recording but that he wouldn't bet on it.

The detached attitude vanished as he felt the first wave of heat from Kruger's fire. He dropped his meat and sprang to the place where his crossbow was lying, snatching up the weapon as though his life depended on his speed. He made no sound, and Kruger, whose attention was focused on building up his fire, did not see what was going on. A struggle that quite literally involved his own life went on behind his back completely without his knowledge.

Dar had actually started to cock his bow when he stopped, one eye on his work and one on the preoccupied human being. For long moments he thought, wavering from one viewpoint to its opposite. Fire was the prime horror of Dar Lang Ahn's life; he had grown up with a terror of it. His people never used it, but lightning or accidental concentration of Arren's rays sometimes caused a blaze. The Teachers and the books had agreed in their endless admonitions to avoid it. It was the end of all life —was the end that would be taken by his own life, naturally, but that was not due for several years yet. Since reaching the edge of the lava field and thereby coming once more within reach of ample food and water, Dar had put his expectation of premature death out of his mind and it was quite a shock to have it brought back so suddenly.

Still, the giant did not seem to have Dar Lang Ahn in mind. Perhaps the fire was merely a part of Kruger's personal and private business, having nothing to do with Dar at all. After all, that would be a rather likely need for someone native to the neighborhood of a volcano. With this thought in his mind Dar relaxed enough to put the crossbow down, though he did not wander very far from the place where he laid it.

He continued to watch the human being, though his attitude bore no resemblance to the lackadaisical one he had shown while the firewood was being gathered. Mentally he was taking notes; the Teachers at the Ice Ramparts would be wanting to put this in a book, beyond all question.

The strange creature had first built his fire up until it was burning quite strongly, then he permitted it to die down until the flames had practically disappeared. A great deal of heat was still being radiated, however, and when it had reached what appeared to be a satisfactory state Kruger startled his companion still more by deliberately exposing his meat to it.

Dar knew that the boy was hungry; he had already formed a fairly exact idea of how much food a human being needed. Why the strange being should proceed to ruin his meal, then, was a mystery of the first order.

When Kruger completed his weird ritual by consuming the meat and then proceeded to extinguish the fire, Dar had long passed his capacity for further surprise. Seeing that the matter was finished he simply rose to his feet and resumed the journey, a sorely puzzled being.

As a matter of fact the notion that the ceremony was over was decidedly erroneous, though it was an error shared by both Dar and Kruger. The latter received the

27

first intimations of the mistake within an hour after completing the meal, and shortly after the first twinges he was rolling helplessly on the ground. Dar, who had seen such symptoms among his own people but could imagine no cause for them this time, could think of nothing to do that might be helpful. Intermittently for more than an hour the cramps continued, giving Kruger just time between attacks to wonder whether he had made his final error in judgment. Eventually his outraged stomach returned the cause of the disturbance and, after a few more admonitory twinges, left him in peace. It was some time, however, before he was really able to give his mind to the problem of why meat which was perfectly wholesome raw should change in such a drastic manner when cooked. Could the smoke given off by the fire have anything to do with it? Perhaps something like the creosote that preserved smoked meat at home—but it would take a well-equipped organic chemistry lab to graduate any of his hypotheses to the theory class. The observed fact was enough for him now—slightly too much, in fact.

The rains had ceased at the usual time after the reappearance of Theer in the south and the temperature was rising again. Each time the red star made another of its odd loops through the sky Kruger wondered whether he would be able to stand the next one. Long months ago he had realized that he could not, at least in the midlatitudes where he had been at the time. On that part of the planet the loops were entirely above the horizon—Theer never set at all. It did, however, vary enormously in apparent size; it was merely Kruger's misfortune that its greatest apparent diameter, and with it the highest temperature of this sweat-box of a planet, occurred while it was at nearly the farthest north point of its loop. The misfortune lay in the fact that, from where he had been left, the loop itself was in the southern half of the sky and to get any part of it below the horizon was obviously best accomplished by going north. There had been, of course, the question of whether he *could* go far enough north; his knowledge of the geography of this world was confined to his memory of what he had seen during the landing orbit. That wasn't much. Still, there had seemed to be nothing to do but take the chance.

He was still not far enough north to be completely out of the red sun's reach, but there seemed a good chance that he might make it. It was now above the horizon for about eight days of its eighteen-day period, if Kruger's watch could still be trusted. He would have been quite happy if the question of Alcyone, which Dar Lang Ahn called Arren, were not forcing itself more and more prominently into his mind. It was all very well to turn a red dwarf sun from a permanent nuisance into an intermittent one, but the advantages tended to disappear when at the same time a blue giant changed from a periodic trouble into a constant fixture. With this matter steadily in the front of his mind Kruger was doing his utmost to get such concepts as temperature into their common language so that he could find out from his companion whether or not there was a spot on the planet which a human being would consider comfortable.

Dar's language was, very slowly, becoming less of a nightmare. As a result a picture was gradually building up in Kruger's mind of the goal that lay ahead of them.

Apparently Dar also wanted a cool place. That information was received by Kruger with unconcealed glee. A catch might lie in what constituted Dar's concept of "cool," but at least he seemed willing to apply the opposite adjectives to their present environment, which was an encouraging sign. Another was the pilot's persistent attempt to describe something which seemed, in the face of all probabilities, to be ice.

Kruger found this theory completely beyond belief at first and kept pestering his companion for a more careful description. However, Dar stuck to his terminology, and finally it occurred to his listener that perhaps the space ship which had brought Dar to Abyormen might

29

be their goal. That should certainly have ice available, at least artificially.

There was the matter of the ocean in their path, whose existence he had gathered earlier. As the boy was not yet sure whether an actual ocean or simply a large lake was involved, he asked whether it would be possible to walk around it. The emphasis which Dar placed on his attempt to express the impossibility of such a move convinced him that "ocean" must be the right word.

It was only at this point that Kruger thought of the possibility of maps. Granting that he had no artistic talent, he should still be able to make a sufficiently good plan of their route together from the lava field to their present position for Dar to grasp what he was trying to do; that would get the word "map" across, and from there on the drawing problem would be Dar Lang Ahn's.

This meant interrupting their journey while the map was drawn, but the effort was an unqualified success. Not only did Dar understand the word and the request that followed its transmission, but he proved to be an excellent cartographer—a natural result of years in the air, since he tended to think of a map as an aerial picture anyway. He made sketch after sketch, clarifying the entire route they were to follow and displaying tremendous knowledge of the planet as a whole.

They were to proceed on their present northeast course until they reached the sea. That was not the closest way to the coast, but it brought them to a point at which a chain of islands stretched across to another continental mass. Getting across the ocean, they would head back along the coast to the left. Kruger assumed that this would be west, but actually it was east; he was already much closer than he realized to Abyormen's north pole, and would pass it before reaching the coast. Dar did not indicate this on his map. They would travel along the new coast for a considerable distance and then head inland. Their journey appeared to terminate shortly thereafter.

Dar indicated a vast area with a satisfied air, said, "Ice!" and sat back as though he had completed a great work. Kruger did not feel quite so happy. He indicated the area the other had just drawn.

"You mean—it's somewhere in this region? Here? or here?"

"Right here." Dar indicated the point at which he had already terminated their course line.

"But what do you mean by the ice all over this place? You can't have ships covering half the planet."

"I don't understand 'ships.' Ice is all over."

"I still don't get it."

Dar had had enough language trouble by this time not to feel particularly exasperated at Kruger's slowness; he proceeded to draw more maps. These were circular, and it quickly became evident that they were views of the whole planet from different directions. His ability to draw such charts was strictly in accord with Kruger's ideas about his origin, so the boy did not feel any surprise from this source. The details did bother him, however.

"You mean that there really is a very big area covered with ice."

"Two of them." Dar indicated his charts. Kruger frowned. Ice caps are noticeable features from space, and he had certainly seen none during the landing. Of course, he was not a trained observer, and had been paying more attention to the behavior of the pilot during the landing maneuver; and Abyormen's atmosphere has its share of clouds. He could quite possibly have missed them for any of those reasons. There was certainly no chance of their having been on the dark side of the planet; at the time of the landing the world's position with respect to the suns was such that there was no dark side.

At any rate the presence of a glacial area was extremely encouraging, particularly right now. The jungle did afford some protection from the approaching Theer which had been lacking on the lava desert, but the higher humidity pretty well offset this advantage. Kruger did not dare discard any more of his clothing because of the ultraviolet light coming from Arren.

As it turned out, he simply had to stop traveling for about fifty hours about the time of Theer's closest approach—the time for which Dar had a phrase in his language, which Kruger naturally translated as "summer." They camped by a stream which the boy hoped would not go dry while they remained, built a shelter whose thatched roof was meant to provide shade and was also kept wet to provide some evaporational cooling, and settled down to wait. Theer's crimson disk, partly visible through the trees, swelled slowly as it moved eastward and slightly higher; continued to swell as it arched across the top of its path and back toward the horizon which Kruger still considered the southeastern one, though his proximity to the pole had made it more like northeast; reached its maximum size, and began visibly to shrink once more before it finally disappeared. It had swung through fully a third of its apparent loop in the sky in only fifty hours, for which Kruger was duly thankful. With its disappearance the journey was resumed.

"Just how sure are you that we are heading toward the part of the coast nearest the island chain?" This question was finally understood.

"I can't be positive, but we're somewhere near right. I've flown over this route a lot."

"You can't be using landmarks, though; we couldn't see anything much smaller than a mountain with all this jungle, and there haven't been any mountains. Couldn't we be working to one side or the other?"

"It is possible but doesn't matter greatly. There are low hills—volcanic cones—along the coast and you can climb one of those if we don't see any islands from the shore." Kruger skipped for the moment the question of why he should be the one to do the climbing.

"But suppose even from a hilltop we can't see any of the island chain. Which way should we travel? Wouldn't it be better to strike for the coast now, so that there'll be no doubt of the direction after we get there?"

"But I don't know the route you suggest."

"You don't know this one, either; you've never walked it before. If your maps are right there's no chance of getting lost, and much less chance than otherwise of wasting time once we reach the coast."

Dar Lang Ahn pondered this bit of wisdom for a few moments and then agreed unreservedly. The course was changed accordingly. All went on as before. It did occur afterward to Dar that perhaps Kruger had been motivated by a desire to get back into a volcanic region sooner.

There were still several hundred miles to go, though Kruger was not sure of this—scale had been one feature left in considerable doubt on Dar's maps. A novelist of the nineteenth century could have made much of every mile of it; the way was made difficult by all the natural characteristics of a rain forest. Undergrowth and swamps delayed them; dangerous animals threatened them; time seemed to stretch onward endlessly and unchangingly. An occasional lava outcrop, usually heavily eroded, served to ease travel for a few miles, but the jungle always returned.

Very gradually, as they advanced, the portion of Theer's loop above the horizon diminished from the eight days near the mudpots to seven, and then to six. Simultaneously the tilt of Arren's diurnal circle changed. On the lava field it had been higher in the south than in the north; now the blue star held nearly even altitude all around the horizon. It was this observation which forced on Kruger's attention the fact that they must be very close to Abyormen's north pole. That, in a way, was good, but in another it bothered him. If they were practically at the pole, where was this ice cap? Or, since Dar stuck to his claim that it was across an ocean in the direction they were traveling, why wasn't it at the pole? Kruger was sure that his problem could be solved in minutes by anyone with the training, but a sixteen-year-old cadet whose planned career involves piloting interstellar vessels simply doesn't get that kind of education.

In any case he was still not absolutely sure that he was interested in the ice cap itself; it seemed likely that Dar's people had simply landed their ship at its edge and Dar was using it as a reference point. The boy was not quite sure what he should do when he got to the ship, but there was no doubt in his mind about the advisability of going there.

All through the long journey the speed and clarity of their conversation improved. The language used was a hodge-podge of the two native tongues involved, but it contained a far larger proportion of Dar's words. This was deliberate on Kruger's part; when he did meet others of Dar's race he wanted to be able to speak to them without needing Dar as an interpreter. Before the pair reached the coast they were talking quite freely, though reiteration and sign language were still frequently necessary; but the basic misunderstanding was still present and seemed less likely than ever to be cleared up. The trouble now was that misunderstandings frequently went unrecognized; each party thought he had expressed himself clearly, or understood perfectly, as the case might be, when actually the thought received was very different from that transmitted. An example of this occurred one day when the question of possible rescue by some of Dar's people had arisen.

"You say that a good many of your people make the same trip in gliders that you were making when you crashed," remarked Kruger. "Mightn't it be a good idea, when we get to the point on the coast that's back under your regular route, to light a smudge fire to attract their attention? We might be saved an awful lot of walking."

"I'm afraid I don't see how attracting their attention would help us, even if you could make a big enough fire to be seen."

"Wouldn't they come down and rescue us?"

"Well—yes, I suppose so. I'm afraid I don't want to reach the Ramparts quite that quickly, though."

In this case, it is possible that the matter might have been cleared up if Kruger had pursued the conversation a little farther, but he had heard Dar speak of the Ramparts earlier and had gathered an impression that when he spoke of the ice region in that way it carried a religious significance which the little pilot was reluctant to discuss. Presumably these trips, then, were scheduled in a fashion which called for Dar's presence only at certain times. Even mishaps such as those the pilot had suffered had their place in the program. This was a far-fetched idea, of course, but it fitted with many of the things Dar Lang Ahn had said and Kruger did not want to offend his little companion. Therefore the subject of the conversation was changed, and Dar assumed that he had explained what would happen, if by some mischance one of his friends were to examine the neighborhood of a fire closely and find Dar Lang Ahn beside it.

"What will you do after getting to the ice?" was Kruger's next question. If that was getting into a dangerous subject he assumed Dar could simply skip any matters he didn't want to discuss.

"There are a few years to go," the other replied calmly. "Twenty-two, if I remember the date correctly. If there is a glider available I suppose I will continue my regular work. If not, then whatever the Teachers say."

Kruger had come to interpret the word "year" as a cycle of the red sun; therefore the time Dar had mentioned was about thirteen months. Before he could ask another question the native put one of his own.

"What will *you* do? Will you actually come all the way to the ice and face the Teachers? I rather thought that you might be planning to stay at the coast when we get there."

"I think it will be more comfortable for me to go on with you as long as you'll let me. They're your people,

35

of course; if you don't want me to see them, that's up to you."

"I very much want you but wasn't sure how you'd face the idea."

"Why should it bother me? I am in worse need of help than you are, and perhaps your Teachers will be willing to give me the assistance I would like. I suppose your group is busy, if you expect to go right back to work, but I can wait. Perhaps after the time you mention is up they'll be free to give me a hand. I'll be willing to do what I can for you folks in the meantime."

Dar did not answer this at once; by the time Kruger knew him well enough to have realized what a shock his words must have caused he had forgotten the details of the conversation. In all likelihood he never did realize Dar's feelings at that moment. The answer was as non-committal a one as the little pilot could manage at the time.

"I'm sure something can be worked out."

The basic misunderstanding was more firmly entrenched than ever, at least on one side.

Nevertheless a personal friendship was growing between the two. At any rate Kruger will swear to this; he knows how he felt about Dar, and has some pretty good evidence on how the alien felt about him. One piece of that evidence came during the journey, at the time they reached the coast—which they finally did, with several of the twenty-two "years" Dar had mentioned used up on the way.

The jungle had thinned somewhat, and patches of lava and volcanic ash were exposed in greater numbers. Evidently the local volcanoes had been active fairly recently as geological phenomena go. There was a great deal more climbing than there had been for some hundreds of miles. None of the elevations was more than a few hundred feet high, but they were frequently fairly steep, the angle of repose for loose volcanic ash is of the order of thirty degrees. Remembering what Dar had said earlier, Kruger suspected that they would come in sight of the sea before very long, but it took him by surprise just the same.

They had reached the brow of one of the hills, apparently just like all the others, when they came to a clearing larger than most which gave them their first real view ahead for many miles. There was plenty to see.

Two fairly large volcanic cones, nearly a thousand feet in height, lay on either side of their course to the north. Between these sparkled a field of intense blue that could only be the body of water they had sought so long. Even this, however, did not claim much of the attention of either traveler. Instead, they both spent several minutes staring at the area between them and the sea—a region nestling in the cleft between the volcanoes and spreading part way up their slopes. Then they turned to each other almost simultaneously and asked, "Your people?"

IV. ARCHAEOLOGY

STRICTLY SPEAKING, there were no people to be seen, but they had rather evidently been there. Cities do not build themselves, and the area between the cones was a city whether seen by human or Abyormenite eyes. None of the buildings seemed very high. Three or four stories, judging by the window arrangement, was the maximum. The windows were apparently quite large—of course, at this distance, small ones would be pretty hard to see—but there was no reflection suggesting that any of them were glazed. This might, of course, be due to chance, but with both suns in the sky and thousands of windows, the chance that none of them would be reflecting light toward the travelers seemed pretty remote.

Kruger realized almost instantly that if his ideas about Dar were correct, such a place would hardly have been made by the pilot's fellows. However, he waited for an answer. This was several seconds in coming; Dar was expecting a reply to his own question. Kruger gave in first.

"No, that place was not built by my people. I have never seen it or anything much like it before."

Dar took this statement with some reservations, but in turn denied any knowledge of the place.

"The shelters at the ice cap are below," he said. "These are built on the surface. My own place, Kwarr, is also on the surface, but the shapes and colors of the buildings are very different. I have never seen a place like this—either." Dar hoped the last word was not too obviously an afterthought.

"The place looks deserted to me. Let's look it over, anyway."

It was here that Dar gave evidence of the friendship he

now felt for the human being. Left to himself, of course, he would have avoided the city by as wide a margin as possible. He was not as happy as he might have been about Kruger's remark concerning the city's deserted state; the Teachers had been rather mysterious about some phases of this fire matter. In spite of his doubts, which came very close to being fears, Dar Lang Ahn made no objection to Kruger's proposal, and the two started down the hill toward the city.

There were several more miles of jungle to pass before they reached it. Dar noted with interest that even the usual animal sounds from the vegetation around them seemed to be lacking. If Kruger noticed this he did not mention it. He might not have noticed it, Dar realized; he had long since learned that his own hearing was considerably more acute than that of his friend. A lack of wild animals might just possibly mean that the city was not as deserted as Kruger believed, and Dar kept his crossbow ready.

No reason to use the weapon developed, however. Eventually the two stood with the jungle behind them and only a few hundred yards of relatively open ground between them and the first buildings. They stopped where they were and examined them carefully.

Still nothing moved and no suspicious sound reached even Dar's ears. After several minutes of waiting Kruger started forward once more. He did not look back or ask whether Dar was following, but the pilot stayed with him —with thoughts quite indescribable to a human being seething in his head. If anything was going to happen— if his illogical trust of Nils Kruger was unjustified—now was the time it would happen. He still held his bow but, to his credit, it was not aimed anywhere near Kruger.

The ground underfoot changed suddenly to firm pavement, on which Dar's claws scraped faintly. Like the buildings, the pavement was made of lava blocks carefully squared and fitted. The buildings were not as high as Kruger had guessed from a distance—that is, not as high in absolute units; they did have the three or four stories that the window arrangement had suggested. Each story, however, averaged about five feet in height.

The buildings themselves hardly constituted houses, at least from Kruger's point of view. They were much too open for that. Not only was more than half the wall space taken up by unglazed windows, but the ground level seemed to consist mostly of doorways. They did have solid roofs and would presumably be some protection against rain, but there their usability as dwelling places seemed to stop.

The doors themselves were a little odd, if they could be called doors. Kruger, after examining the outside of half a dozen buildings, found himself unable to decide whether the lower stories could be said to have a bell-shaped door every few feet, or that the outer walls consisted of oddly shaped pillars. The latter seemed a slightly better way to put it, since calling an opening four feet wide at the bottom, three and a half feet high, and shaped like a probability curve a "door" seemed stretching the usual meaning of the word.

Both travelers realized one thing rather quickly; each had been telling the truth in denying any connection with the city. The ceilings were too low for human beings, and while Dar could have moved about inside any one chamber without trouble, the doors had certainly not been built for his species either. This realization almost made Dar uncock his weapon—but not quite.

Kruger wanted to investigate the interiors of some of the buildings, but at Dar's suggestion decided to get a better idea of the entire city first. They moved on down the street on which they had found themselves when they first reached pavement.

This led toward the sea but did not appear to reach it. The plan of the city was sufficiently complicated so that no one street appeared to go entirely across it. Kruger kept on toward the sea, believing that the largest and most informative buildings should be at the waterfront.

He was partly right. The city did extend down to the sea, with more imposing structures appearing as they proceeded. However, the largest of these were not at the waterfront. They were well out in the harbor.

It took some little time for Kruger to digest this fact. Dar was even more startled; he had been willing to accept evidence that Kruger had no connection with the builders of this city, but he had been perfectly sure that the builders themselves were fire-lovers—the location as well as the structural materials used seemed to prove that. Such a hypothesis, however, did not square too well with buildings seemingly built under water with complete disregard of the change of environment. Dar knew little about fire, but even he was aware of this inconsistency. He drew a little closer to his large friend.

"I guess this place must be older than I thought," Kruger remarked slowly. "It must have taken a long time to drop the coast or raise the water level enough to submerge those buildings. It couldn't have been a sudden shock or the place wouldn't be standing."

"What are we going to do, then?"

"Well, I'd still like to go through one of these buildings. There's no telling what we'll find that might prove useful, and anyway I'm curious."

Dar found that he was curious too, in spite of the weight of eight centuries of tradition, and he followed Kruger without objection as the boy walked over to a nearby building, dropped to his hands and knees, and crawled through one of the openings in the wall. Inside, Dar was able to stand up with reasonable head clearance; he walked around freely while Kruger remained on his knees for some time looking about him.

The open structure of the outer wall had the advantage of letting in plenty of light, but it also meant that they had seen most of what there was to see from outside. In this case that was very little. A room, or hallway, about fifteen feet wide ran the full length of the building parallel to the street; it was completely devoid of furnishings

41

of any sort. The inner wall of this passage possessed doors similar in size and shape to those leading from the street but not nearly so many of them. Kruger chose one at random and crawled through. Dar followed.

This room was also long and narrow, but its longer dimension was away from the street rather than parallel to it; the door through which they had entered was in one end. It was much smaller than the outer hall. At far end was a dais raised about a foot from the floor. At four points, seemingly at random, on the floor itself were dome-shaped structures about two feet high and eighteen inches in diameter with fluted sides that made them look like inverted jelly-molds. They were made of some light-colored stone; Kruger was just barely able to slide one along the floor when he got between it and the wall and used his legs. Their purpose was certainly not obvious. Other furniture seemed easier to explain; there was a rectangular metal affair with sliding drawers and a mirror-smooth surface made of highly polished obsidian set into one of the side walls. The mirror, if that was its intended function, was about the same size and shape as the doors.

The drawers of the bureau, or filing cabinet, or whatever it was were fastened by simple latches. The top one was empty. The second was nearly full of metal objects, about half of which had no obvious function, while the others might very well have been drawing instruments. There was a pair of dividers, a straight edge marked off as a scale, a semicircular protractor divided into eighteen major parts by deep engraving in the metal, and several tools apparently for both cutting and engraving. One of these, a scalpel-like affair with a double-edged blade and a handle about three inches long, he pointed out to Dar with the suggestion that he take it along; he had been using Kruger's knife on his meat ever since he had discovered the advantages of a metal blade. The handle was not of a shape to fit his hand very closely, but neither was that of Kruger's knife, and this at least was nearer to the proper size.

Further examination of the room disclosed a small pipe emerging from one wall, with what appeared to be a burner nozzle at the tip. Kruger deduced a gas lighting fixture, with the corollary that the builders of the city possessed eyes.

The dais at the rear of the room contained two shallow, bowl-shaped depressions a little under four feet in diameter which might have been flower pots or bathtubs for all Kruger could guess. Approaching it, however, he seemed to feel an increase in temperature. Since he was always soaked with perspiration anyway, he wasn't sure at first, but when he touched the wall he jerked his hand away again with a startled exclamation; the surface was burning hot.

Dar preserved himself from hysterics only by a major exercise of will. He wanted nothing to do with sources of heat, artificial or not, and he withdrew to the door while Kruger finished his investigations alone. These took some time, for just as he had decided that there was nothing more to see, his eye caught a metal plate set flush with the floor. This was only about an inch square, and almost featureless, but careful examination disclosed a pair of tiny perforations near each of its sides.

Kruger went back to the drawer that held the drawing instruments, secured the dividers, and by inserting their points in two of the holes finally managed to pry up the plate. Its metal took no visible damage from what was presumably unorthodox treatment. This fact, however, did not hold Kruger's attention at the time.

What caught his eye was simple enough—merely a dull-colored surface with two small holes. After regarding these silently for several seconds Kruger went to work once more with his improvised pry-bar, and in a few minutes the dull plate came out beside its cover. Underneath it was exactly what the boy had expected to see—two silvery wires surrounded and separated by a black, flexible coating and leading to metal cups. With all due respect to the possibilities inherent in different culture backgrounds Kruger felt safe in concluding that he had been dissecting a plug receptacle designed to deliver current to whatever the inhabitant of the room chose. In short, an electric socket.

He looked at the wires, and up to the pipe and jet on the wall, and back to the wires, whistling tunelessly. Then he replaced the covers and relieved Dar's mind by leaving the room.

Kruger was not frightened but was sorely puzzled by what he had seen. A city, still in good repair although without any present inhabitants, presumably abandoned not long ago—yet running down into the ocean for a distance that implied centuries of land sinking, equipped with gas-lighting and electric wiring in the same building.

Dar was not able to throw light on the question. He recognized the weight of his friend's arguments in all matters except the gas-electricity question and was willing to accept a qualified opinion there. Kruger explained that situation as well as he could while they rested in the shade of the building's entrance hall. Theer was practically at his closest, and travel was impractical anyway. Dar understood without any trouble that a gas light was a form of fire and led the conversation hastily on to the question of electricity. Kruger did not expect to get much of this concept across and was pleasantly surprised to discover that Dar appeared to be following quite well. The explanation was long, of course, but by the time Theer had dropped once more behind the hills the boy was as sure as he ever became that he was understood.

The question then arose of just what they should do about it all. Kruger thought it would be best for them to examine at least one or two more buildings to make sure that the one they had seen was typical; then they would have some more or less organized information, which Dar could give to his people. Kruger's chance to report it to *his* people seemed a good deal more remote, but perhaps he could use the knowledge himself.

Dar had a more serious problem. His interest had been

aroused, of course; he would like, in one way, to bring a group of his people and perhaps some Teachers back to this place so that they could learn more about the electricity that Kruger had described. At the same time there was the fact that he had violated firm and long-standing instructions—not merely orders of the Teachers but written material handed down in books from the time before his people were born—against having anything to do with fire. There could be no doubt that whoever had built this place had never heard of those laws. If Dar made a complete report at the Ice Ramparts would the result be an expedition, or censure? This was his problem, of course; he could not ask Kruger for advice. The human being obviously had never heard of the law either but could hardly be blamed for that; his background was different.

Still, what he was to do with the information made little difference in what he should do now about acquiring more. He followed Kruger's lead, therefore, and some hours were spent in going through a number of the structures.

These were no more identical than the buildings of a terrestrial city would have been, but none of the variations were particularly startling. The gas pipe-electric wiring anomaly seemed to exist everywhere; Dar pointed out that the pipes were only in inner rooms, whereas electrical outlets frequently appeared in entrance halls and even on outer walls. There seemed to be some prejudice on the part of the city dwellers against the use of electricity for lighting. Kruger refused to credit Dar's suggestion that they might not have invented electric lights. His opinion was that anyone who could construct a dependable current source, sufficient for a city, could at least strike an arc with it. He may have been right.

Although Theer had not been down very long, several thunder showers had passed over the city while they were investigating. When the two decided that they had seen enough and should probably continue their journey they found that another of the storms was just breaking. It would not have been impossible to travel in the rain—Kruger was usually soaking wet anyway—but visibility was not good and they decided to wait.

Like most of the others the shower did not last too long, and presently the sky began to lighten. Dar replaced his pack on his shoulders and they started out while rain was still hissing down. It struck the pavement loudly enough to make conversation difficult, and rivulets of water gurgled down the slope of the gutterless street toward the sea. Probably this was what kept Dar's ears from warning them. At any rate that was what he claimed later.

Whatever the reason, neither of them knew they were not alone until the company showed itself deliberately. The interruption to their journey involved both word and action; the word was "Stop!" and the action took the form of a crossbow bolt which splintered against the street in front of them. Dar and Kruger, realizing that the projectile must have come from above, rapidly covered with their eyes the roof edges in their vicinity, but nothing moved.

The word had been in Dar's language, so the pilot took it on himself to answer. He very carefully refrained from raising his own crossbow. "What do you want?"

"You must come with us."

"Why?" Kruger had understood enough of the foregoing conversation to be able to ask this question.

"You are ——— ——— ——— the city." The first and last parts of this sentence were all the boy could follow.

"What's their trouble?" asked Kruger.

"The trouble is ours. We are—we did—coming in the city was bad."

"Why?"

"They do not say." Dar did not mention that he thought he knew; this was no time for lengthy explanations.

"Do you have any ideas as to who these are?"

"Ideas, but I don't know."

"What do you think we should do?"

46

"What they say." Dar, standing in the middle of a bare street, was in no mood for a crossbow duel with an unknown number of antagonists, all under excellent cover. Nevertheless there was one question in his mind.

"What will be done to us for entering your city?"

"Whatever the Teachers say. It is not for us to decide."

"What has happened in the past?"

"No one has disobeyed a Teacher for many years. At first, when people were young, some did; they suffered, and did not offend again."

"But suppose we did not know we were offending?"

"You must have known; you are a person. The thing with you may be forgiven. The Teachers will decide."

"But I never heard of this place; my Teachers never told me of it, and it is not in the books. How could I know?"

"You must have very stupid Teachers. Maybe you will not be blamed for that." Dar was sufficiently indignant to make a retort which Kruger would have discouraged, had he been able to follow the conversation at all closely.

"Am I from your city?"

"No."

"Did your Teachers tell you of my city?"

"No."

"Then there must be two sets of stupid Teachers on Abyormen." If Kruger had understood this remark he would have confidently expected to see it answered with a volley of crossbow bolts, but nothing of the sort happened. The unseen speaker simply returned to the original question.

"Will you come with us without fighting?"

"We will come." Dar made the answer without any further consultation with Kruger. After all, the boy had already asked Dar what should be done, and presumably had no opinion of his own.

With Dar Lang Ahn's words the openings in the surrounding buildings gave forth some fifty beings. Kruger was able to take the revelation without particular surprise, but Dar was shocked beyond measure to find that the attackers were identical physically with himself. He was a well-traveled individual; he had met, on his official trips to the Ice Ramparts and elsewhere, members of his race from several score cities scattered over Abyormen's globe, and he had never heard of any except the uncaught savages living out of touch with the Teacher-ruled cities. Still, there was no questioning the facts; the beings surrounding him might have come straight from any city he had visited. Even the carrying harness they wore was virtually identical with his own, and the crossbows borne by most of them might have been made by Merr Kra Lar, home in Kwarr.

One who seemed to be in charge spoke as soon as he came up to them.

"You used a word that I never heard a little while ago. What is a book?" This question was not understood by Kruger; Dar had never told him what was in the pack he kept so carefully by him. Dar might not have been surprised at his human companion's ignorance of such matters, but that a member of his own species should never have heard of a book was quite unthinkable. Life could not go on without a record of the life that had gone before!

When he recovered from the astonishment that the question had caused him he tried to explain, but his listener seemed unable to digest the concept of writing. In an effort to clarify the point Dar removed one of the books from his pack and held it open before him while he tried to explain the significance of the marks, but this produced a result he had not foreseen.

"I do not quite understand why you need such a thing when you can ask Teachers for what you need to know, but perhaps our Teachers can tell why you do. We will show them your books; give them to me."

V. CONFISCATION

THERE WAS NOTHING else to do; one crossbow can do nothing against two-score. For an instant Dar thought of making a wild break through the surrounding group to the shelter of the nearest building, but he abandoned the idea. Alive, he might recover the books.

"I would prefer to carry them and show them to your Teachers myself," he suggested.

"There is no need to bring you to them at all unless they order it," was the reply, "but they will certainly want to see your books. I will go to them and show them the books and ask what is to be done to you."

"But I want to see them, to explain why I did not know I was breaking their law."

"I will tell them that. Since you have broken it what you want is not important."

"But won't they want to see my companion? You have already said he was different from people."

"Yes, I will take him."

"Then you will need me. He knows very little proper speech, and I know some of his words."

"If the Teachers wish to speak as well as look, and find that they need your aid, you will be sent for." The speaker held out a hand and Dar reluctantly handed over his priceless pack.

Marching orders were given and the group headed back the way Dar and Kruger had come. However, instead of turning inland when they reached the avenue the pair had followed to the sea, they crossed it and headed toward the seaward side of one of the volcanoes—the one that had been on the left as the wanderers approached the city.

49

For the first time Dar regretted that he had not insisted on learning more of Kruger's language. The problem was to get the books back and get out of reach of these people, the sooner the better; failing that, to get out himself and get a report to the Ice Ramparts telling of their location. That *had* to be done in less than twenty years; no alternative was thinkable. With luck, Nils Kruger would help. Just now it would hardly be advisable to discuss the matter with him; too many of the words they would have to use would be understood by those surrounding them. Later, perhaps they would be left alone; if not, Dar would simply have to make use of the little English he had mastered. In that connection an idea struck him and he spoke to Kruger, using his English vocabulary to the utmost.

"Nils, talk while going. Your tongue. About anything." He could not be more explicit; he wanted Kruger to discuss what they saw as they went along, in the hope that an occasional word would bear a sufficiently obvious meaning, when considered in connection with the words Dar already knew, for the native to grasp it. Kruger did not understand this, but he could see that Dar had something definite in mind, and endeavored to please. Since the most obvious subject for speech was just what Dar wanted, things did not go too badly.

It was a method which would not have been very practical, used by most human beings, but with the sort of memory Dar possessed it was not completely unreasonable. Even so, the little pilot's vocabulary increased very, very slowly indeed and frequently had to be corrected.

While this was going on the group passed the volcano, following the narrow beach of pulverized ash between it and the sea. On the other side the jungle came down practically to the shore in scattered tufts of vegetation, separated by piles of ejecta and occasional small sheets of lava. For a couple of hours they threaded their way through these patches of jungle, gradually working away from the sea. The ground did not rise again; they remained about

50

at sea level and Kruger would not have been surprised to encounter another swamp. Instead they finally ran into a region of fog.

This was the first time in his months on Abyormen that Kruger had encountered this phenomenon and he was more than a little surprised. It did not seem to go with the air temperature. Nevertheless the drifting wisps of water vapor were there and as the group advanced they grew larger and more frequent. The boy had a sufficiently good background of physics to attribute the whole thing to one of two causes—either something cooling the nearly saturated air, or a body of water whose temperature was higher than that of the air above it. He was not too startled, therefore, when the second of these situations materialized. Pools of water appeared on both sides of their path, and presently the way led into a clearing two or three hundred yards across, dotted with more bodies of water which were giving off thick plumes of vapor. Some were bubbling violently, others lying quiet in the sunlight, but all seemed to be hot. Dar was visibly nervous —visibly to their captors, that is; Kruger still did not recognize the symptoms. The being who carried the pack was moved to inquire about it.

"Has your companion said something to trouble you?"

"No," replied Dar, "but it seems to me that if anyone is trespassing on forbidden ground, it is this group, right now."

"Why? No one has forbidden this area; we were told to live here."

"By your Teachers?"

"Of course."

"With all this smoke?"

"It is water-smoke; it hurts no one. See, your friend is not bothered by it."

Kruger had stepped aside to one of the hot pools, watched alertly but not prevented by his captors, and was examining both the water and the rock around it carefully. Up to now he had seen no limestone on the planet, but this pool was rimmed with travertine. The rim was a foot or so higher than the rock a short distance away.

Kruger looked over these factors and nodded to himself. Then he turned back to the rest—his captors had stopped, with remarkable complaisance, to let him finish his examination—and asked the individual with the pack, "How often do these————?" He had no word for the verb he wanted, but swung his hands up and outward in a fashion that was clear to everyone but Dar. The leader answered without apparent hesitation.

"No law. Sometimes once in two or three years, sometimes two or three dozen times a year."

"How high?"

"Sometimes just overflows, sometimes tree-high. Lots of noise, lots of steam."

There was nothing surprising, of course, about geysers in a volcanic area. However, Kruger had an impression that savage and semicivilized races usually avoided them, and he spent some time wondering whether the answer he had received told him anything about these beings. He decided ruefully that for practical purposes it didn't.

By the time he had reached this conclusion the journey was almost over. They had crossed the clearing where the geysers were located, and in the jungle on the far side was a collection of structures which proved to be the "city" of their captors. It told a good deal more about the creatures than their words had.

The buildings were plain thatched huts, somewhat more complicated than the ones Kruger had built during the midsummer seasons along their route but much simpler than some that may be found in African kraals. The leader called out as they approached the village, and what turned out to be the rest of the population emerged from the huts to see them arrive.

Kruger had read his share of adventure novels and acquired most of what he thought he knew of primitive races from these. As a result he became distinctly uneasy about one aspect of the crowd which gathered about the captives. They were all the same size, as nearly as his eye could distinguish. The first impression this gave the boy was that this was a war party, with women and children strictly left at home. He relaxed slightly when he saw that only those who had been in the party that captured him and Dar were armed. However, the silence of the newcomers rather affected him after a while. Logically, they should all have been asking questions about the captives; instead they were merely staring at Kruger.

It was Dar who broke the silence, not because he particularly minded being ignored in the circumstances but because he was worried about his books.

"Well, when do we see these Teachers of yours?" he asked. The eyes of the being who had the pack swiveled toward him.

"When they say. We plan to eat first, but while food is being prepared I will report our return to them."

One of the people who had not been with the party spoke up. "It is reported; we heard you coming and could tell by the alien's voice that you had succeeded."

Kruger understood enough of this sentence to see why the villagers were less surprised at their arrival than might have been expected. The party must have been sent out to capture the wanderers; Dar and he must have been seen crossing the clearing to the city. The times involved were reasonable.

"The Teacher who answered said that the party and the captives might eat and that both captives were then to be brought to him." Neither Kruger nor Dar made any objection to this, though the boy had his usual doubts about the food.

Some of it, which was served first, was vegetation; it came in great baskets which were placed on the ground. Everyone sat around them and helped himself, so Kruger had no difficulty in selecting what he knew to be safe for him. While this was going on, however, a number of villagers had gone out to the geysers carrying other baskets containing cuts of meat. They returned with these and

53

replaced the empty vegetable containers with those they had carried, and Kruger found to his dismay that the meat was hot—too hot to handle comfortably. Apparently it had been cooked in one of the springs.

Both he and Dar were still hungry, but neither dared try the meat after Kruger's earlier experience. They watched gloomily while the villagers gulped it down, until a point struck the boy.

"Dar, these people are the same as you. The cooking doesn't spoil the food for them; why don't you eat, at least? One of us should keep his strength up." Dar was a little doubtful about his identity with the villagers, but the other point touched his sense of duty and after wrestling with his conscience for a few moments he agreed that his friend was right. His uneasiness as he ate was clear to the people around him and seemed to cause more surprise than Kruger's appearance had done.

Inevitably, he was asked what the trouble was and the surprised eyes turned back to Kruger as Dar related his unfortunate experience with cooked meat.

"I do not understand how that can be," remarked one of the villagers. "We have always cooked our meat; it is the rule. Perhaps your friend used a spring which had poison in the water."

"He did not use a spring at all. There was only the river, which was cold, and we had nothing to hold water—at least, nothing big enough."

"Then how could he possibly have cooked the meat?"

"He held it over a fire."

The sudden buzz of conversation which greeted this word seemed to Dar to represent the first reasonable reaction he had obtained from these people, but he quickly found that he had been misunderstood.

"Was the fire near here?" was the next question. "We are ordered to tell the Teachers whenever a volcano other than the ones near the Great City becomes active."

"It was not a volcano. He made the fire himself." The eyes swiveled back to Nils Kruger and a dead silence ensued. No one asked Dar to repeat his words; the average Abyormenite had too much confidence in his own hearing and memory to suppose that he might have misunderstood such a simple sentence. There was a distinct atmosphere of disbelief, however. Dar would almost have wagered his books on the question that would come next. He would have won.

"How is this done? He looks strange but not powerful." The last word did not mean purely physical power; it was a general term covering all sorts of ability.

"He has a device which makes a very tiny fire when he touches it properly. With this he lights small bits of wood and when these burn he uses them to light larger ones."

The creature had doubts. So did most of the others; there was a general grunt of agreement when he said, "I will have to see this." Dar carefully refrained from giving openly his equivalent of a smile.

"Will your Teachers be willing to wait until he has shown you, or should this thing be shown to them also?" This question caused some rapid discussion among the villagers, which culminated in a rapid journey by one of them to a small hut which stood near one side of the cluster of dwellings. Dar watched with interest as the fellow disappeared inside, and endeavored to decipher the faint mutters of speech that came out. He failed in this attempt and had to await the messenger's return.

"The Teacher says to bring wood, such as the strange one needs, and let him see the building of the fire." The natives scattered at once to their huts, while Dar filled Kruger in on the numerous items he had missed in the conversation. By the time this was accomplished wood was arriving from all directions.

None of it had come straight from the jungle; it had evidently been cut some time before and been drying in the huts. There was no reason from the shape of the pieces to suppose that it had been originally obtained for firewood, and every reason from the background of the people to suppose that it had not, but there it was. Kruger selected a few pieces and shaved them into slivers with his knife, then made up a small armful of larger material and stood up, signifying that he was ready. Dar started to lead the way toward the hut where the messenger had gone.

Instantly he was interrupted.

"Not that way, stranger!"

"But is not that where your Teachers are?"

"In a little place like that? Certainly not. They *talk* there, it is true, but they wish to *see* you and your fire-maker. Come this way." The speaker started to retrace the path by which they had come to the village and the prisoners followed him. The rest of the population trailed along.

A well-marked path wound among the hot springs. The captives followed it toward an unusually large pool near the side of the clearing away from the now distant sea. Apparently this one overflowed more frequently than the others or else had a greater supply of mineral in whatever subterranean source it sprang from, for its edge was nearly three feet high. The water within the rim steamed and bubbled furiously.

The area around the pool was clear except at one point, where an object that looked like a detached lump of travertine projected from the rim. It was dome-shaped except for the flattened top and was about as high as the rim and perhaps five feet in diameter. Its surface was mostly smooth, but there were a number of deep pits scattered around its sides.

Kruger would not have looked at it twice, except for the fact that they were stopped in front of it and the entire population of the village gathered around. This caused the boy to examine the outcrop more closely and he decided that someone had done a rather skillful bit of masonry. Presumably the Teachers were inside; the small holes must serve as spy-ports and ventilators. No entrance was visible. Perhaps it was inside the pool rim, where he could not see, or even some distance away and connected by a tunnel. He was not surprised to hear a voice come from the mound of stone.

"Who are you?" The question was not ambiguous; the grammatical arrangements of the language left no doubt that Kruger was the one addressed. For an instant the boy was not sure how to answer, then he decided simply to tell the truth.

"I am Nils Kruger, pilot-cadet of the cruiser *Alphard*." He had to translate the nouns into similes in the Abyormenite language but was reasonably satisfied with the job. The next question made him wonder whether he was doing the right thing, however.

"When do you die?"

Kruger found himself at a slight loss for an answer to this question. It seemed to be nothing but a simple, straightforward one about how long he had to live, but he found himself unable to answer it.

"I do not know," was the only response he could give. This led to a silence from the stone at least as long as the one his own hesitation had caused. With the next words the hidden speaker gave the impression of one who has shelved, for the time at least, a puzzling subject.

"You are supposed to be able to make fire. Do so." Kruger, completely at a loss as to where he stood with the invisible questioner, obeyed. There was no difficulty to the job; the wood was dry and Arren furnished all the radiation the little battery needed. The snap of the high-tension sparks sent the nearer villagers back in momentary alarm, though to Kruger it sounded much like Dar's crossbow. The shavings caught instantly and sixty seconds later a very respectable little fire was blazing on the stone a few yards from the rock shelter of the Teachers. Throughout the operation questions had kept coming and Kruger had been answering them: why the wood had to be small at first, why he had chosen wood that was dry, and what was the source of the sparks. The answering was extremely difficult. Kruger faced roughly the same problem as would a high-school student asked to give a lecture on high-school-level physics or chemistry in French after perhaps a year's study of the language. As a result he was still trying to improvise signs and words when the fire burned out.

The creature within the rock shelter finally satisfied himself on fires—or, more probably, on what Kruger knew about them—and proceeded to a matter which seemed to interest him more.

"Are you from another world traveling about Theer, or from one circling Arren?"

Dar simply did not understand, but Kruger understood much too well. He was thunderstruck, after the usual fashion of human beings who find their pet theories suddenly untenable.

"Witch-doctor my eye!" he muttered under his breath, but was able to think of no coherent answer for the moment.

"What was that?" Kruger had forgotten for a moment that hyper-acute hearing seemed rather common on this world.

"An expression of surprise, in my own language," he answered hastily. "I do not think I understood your question."

"I think you did." Unhuman though the accents were Kruger had a sudden picture of a stern schoolmaster on the other side of the barrier, and decided that he might as well continue his policy of frankness.

"No, I do not come from Arren; I do not even know whether it has any planets, and Theer has no others." The listener accepted the new word without comment; its meaning must have been obvious enough from context. "My home world travels about a sun much fainter than Arren, but much brighter than Theer, whose distance from this system I cannot give in your language."

"Then there are other suns?"

"Yes."

"Why did you come here?"

"We were exploring—learning what other worlds and their suns were like."

"Why are you alone?"

Kruger related in detail the accident that had dropped his space-suited form into a mud pot, the natural conclusion of his friends that he had perished, and his survival by means of a fortuitous tree root.

"When will your people return?"

"I do not expect them back at all. They had no reason to believe this world had inhabitants; the cities of Dar's people, which he has told me about, were not seen, and the village of these people of yours could not possibly have been detected. In any case the ship was on a survey trip which would last for quite a number of your years, and it might be fully as long after it returned home before the data on this system was even examined. Even then there will be no particular reason to come back; there is much to do a great deal closer to home."

"Then to your people you are dead already."

"Yes, I'm afraid so."

"Do you know how your flying vessels work?" Kruger hesitated at this question, then remembered that he had described himself already as a pilot cadet.

"I know the forces and technology involved, yes."

"Then why have you not tried to build one and return to your world?"

"Knowledge and ability are two different things. I know how this world came into being, but couldn't do the job myself."

"Why are you with this one you call Dar?"

"I met him. Two people can get along better than one. Also, I was looking for a place on this world cool enough for a human being, and he said something about an ice cap to which he was going. That was enough for me."

"What would you do about others of his kind if you met them at this ice cap?"

"Endeavor to get along with them, I suppose. In a way, they'd be the only people I'd have; I'd treat them

59

as mine, if they'd allow it." There was a pause after this answer, as though the hidden Teachers were conferring or considering. Then the questions resumed, but this time were directed at Dar Lang Ahn.

In reply, he stated that he was a pilot, normally assigned to the route between the city of Kwarr and the Ice Ramparts. The questioners asked for the location of the city, which Dar had to describe in great detail. He and Kruger both wondered whether the Teachers were really ignorant of it, or testing Dar's veracity.

No suggestion was made that Dar was not a native of the planet, and as the questioning went on Kruger grew more and more puzzled. It was some time before it occurred to him that since Dar was obviously of the same species as these people they must also be from another world. Why they were living as near-savages on this one was a mystery, but perhaps they had been marooned through damage to their ship. That would account for the questions about his own ability to build a space flier. In fact, for a moment it seemed to account for everything except why the "Teachers" remained in concealment.

"What are these 'books' you were carrying and about which you seem so anxious?" This question snapped Kruger's wandering attention back to the present. He had been wanting to ask the same thing for some time.

"They are the records of what our people have learned and done during their lives. The records which came down to us from those who went before were returned to safety at the Ramparts long ago, after we had learned what they contained, but it is the law that each people shall make its own books, as well, which must then be saved as those made before have been."

"I see. An interesting idea; we shall have to consider it further. Now, another matter: you have given some of our people the impression that you consider it unlawful to have dealings with fire. Is that correct?"

"Yes."

"Why?"

"Our Teachers have told us, and our books from times past have said the same."

"Did they say it would kill you?"

"There was that, but it was something more. Being killed is one thing—we all die when the time comes, anyway—but this seemed to be something worse. I guess you're deader when you die from heat, or something. Neither the Teachers nor the books ever made it very clear."

"Yet you accompany this being who makes fires whenever he wishes."

"It worried me at first, but I decided that since he is not a real person he must have a different set of laws. I felt that bringing information about him back to my people at the Ice Ramparts would outweigh any violations I might commit in other directions. Besides, I kept as far as possible from the fires he made."

There was another fairly lengthy silence before the Teacher spoke again. When he did, his tone and words were quite encouraging at first.

"You have been informative, cooperative, and helpful —both of you," the hidden being said. "We appreciate it; therefore we thank you.

"You will remain with our people for the time being. They will see that you are comfortable and fed; I fear we can do nothing now about the coolness the alien wants, but even that may be arranged in time.

"Place the books and the fire-lighting machine on the stone, and let everyone depart."

VI. INVESTIGATION

A PERIOD of alternating rain and sunshine and the brief return and departure of Theer left the two travelers with the impression that the "Teachers" of the tribe which had captured them might be well disposed but were rather opinionated beings. When they said anything it was so. Unfortunately they had said that Nils Kruger and Dar Lang Ahn should remain available for talk, and the village of creatures who obeyed them implicitly were quite able to make it so.

Actually they were not completely prisoners. They could wander where they pleased within the village and its immediate environs, except into the hut where villagers went to talk to the Teachers. Also, when the unseen beings learned about Kruger's watch, which was during the second interview, they quite obligingly agreed that the two need not even remain nearby, provided that they appear at certain regular intervals which were determined by mutual agreement on the spot. There was, Kruger realized, some pretty good psychology at work; at the same time this freedom was granted, a half-promise was made to Dar that his books would be returned before too long—the time was left vague. "Just now they were being examined with great interest." Kruger noted that no request was made for Dar to give lessons in his written language, but the important fact was that Dar was chained to the neighborhood by that promise as securely as though metallic shackles had been used. He refused to consider for a moment any suggestion which involved deserting his precious books.

More as an experiment than anything else, Kruger

asked on one occasion whether the law of the village forbidding entrance to the city applied to the captives. He expected a curt refusal and was pleasantly surprised when they were allowed to go there, on condition that nothing was removed or injured. He said nothing about the knife that Dar had appropriated and cheerfully made the required promise.

Dar was afraid that the villagers would resent this; it did seem a little odd, permitting the captives to do something that was illegal for the captors. However, no sign of such a feeling appeared and they finally concluded that the word of the Teachers must be the absolutely final authority for these people.

They took advantage of their permission several times, but found nothing more surprising than the things that had turned up during their first inspection. Kruger made a careful and well-planned search for the generating station that supplied power to the city wiring, but failed to find it. He was disappointed; he would have liked very much to know what the source of power of the city builders might have been.

The Teachers never asked how closely their condition was being followed, though one day the two had a bad scare during one of the conversations.

"Dar," the speaker had asked, "what is the substance of which those harness buckles of yours are made?" The pilot appeared not to be bothered by the question, but Kruger suddenly realized what might lie behind it and answered hastily, "He had them before we came; they did not come from the city."

"We realize that," came the answer, "but that is not what we wanted to know. Dar?"

"They are of iron," the pilot replied, truthfully.

"So we thought. Would you mind explaining how a person who is forbidden to have anything to do with fire, and whose people all live under the same law, came by such articles?"

"I can tell, but not explain," Dar answered precisely.

"I found them. A great deal of such material was found near and in the city when we first lived. We took what we wanted of it, since there was no law forbidding it. I did not know that iron had any connection with fire." He looked uneasily down at the buckles.

This conversation ended there; as a matter of fact it was violently interrupted. One of the geysers a scant thirty yards from where the prisoners sat chose this moment to release some of its energy, and large quantities of boiling water began to appear. Dar and Kruger did not wait to say any farewells; they went, straight away from the disturbance and as rapidly as the clouds of vapor permitted.

Twice Kruger tripped over irregularities in the rock; both times he struggled back to his feet with scalding water almost on him. For what seemed to them both like hours, but which probably was rather less than a minute, no thought entered either of their minds except that of self-preservation; then they were safely beyond the reach of the disturbance.

Immediately, the instant they were sure of this, the two stopped; they both had the same thought, but it no longer dealt with their own safety. For a full hour, until long after the vapor had cleared away, they waited and watched, hoping to get a glimpse of the Teachers who would presumably have been driven out in the same way as their captives. Nothing moved in all that time, however, and when the clearing of the air was complete they could see the dome of rock sitting apparently unchanged with no sign that anyone or anything had moved in its vicinity. They went back and circled the pool beside which it lay, so as to see it from every side, for now if ever the entrance would be visible, but they found nothing

Both were a trifle surprised when, on their return after the usual interval, discussion went on as though nothing had happened. Kruger wished he dared ask how the Teachers had escaped, but somehow failed to bring himself to the point of actually raising the question.

By this time he had told a good deal about his people. Dar had done the same. Kruger's facility with the language had grown far more rapidly than in any similar period of his companionship with Dar alone.

Dar, by this time, had realized his original error about Kruger, though his ideas of astronomy were distinctly sketchy. The boy, however, was by no means convinced that Dar and the villagers were natives of the planet; the Teachers had always shied away from direct answers on that subject and there was no direct evidence which tended to disprove the original notion that they were maroons like himself—none, at least, that Kruger recognized as such.

Their stay in the village was not entirely composed of exploration and conversation. Several times life became fairly exciting, in fact. On one occasion Kruger fell into a concealed pit which had rather obviously been made to trap animals; only the fact that it seemed to have been made for rather large game enabled him to miss the sharpened stake in the bottom. Again, while leaving a building at one edge of the city well up the side of one of the volcanoes, Kruger and Dar were nearly engulfed by a slide of volcanic ash which had apparently been loosened by recent rain. They had ducked back into the building barely in time, and afterward had to make their way painfully—for Kruger, that is—through the structure to find an exit on the other side, the uphill doors having been completely blocked.

Several times Dar renewed his request for the return of the books; his time was running out, in more senses than one. The Teachers still professed interest in the volumes, however, and failed to give any definite time when the interest might be expected to wane.

Several times when he and Dar were alone Kruger suggested, more or less forcefully, that they simply fail to return to the village some day, get to the Ice Ramparts, and return with enough assistance to compel the return of Dar's property; but the pilot refused to leave. It took a fairly complex combination of circumstances to change his mind.

They had covered the greater part of the city which lay toward the village but had done virtually nothing with the other side. Actually there was little reason to suppose that it would provide anything they had not seen already, and even Kruger was getting a little weary of rambling through deserted buildings, when Dar noticed that one street seemed to lead off from the farther side of the city around the second volcano, which they had never reached. This street was not noticeable from sea level; Dar saw it from the edge of the city well up the other hill—quite close, in fact, to the place where they had nearly been buried. The two decided to investigate immediately.

It took some time to descend one volcano, cross the level portion of the city, and climb the other to the point which Dar's memory indicated as being the start of the street in question; when they reached it, enough time had passed to suggest that they might possibly be late for their next conversation with the Teachers. They had always been careful not to overstay their leave, feeling quite logically that their freedom might suffer should they do so, but this time they decided to take the chance.

The street went up the hill rather steeply, angling at first toward the seaward side of the cone. From below they had not been able to tell whether it formed a switchback leading to the top of the volcano or a spiral going around it; they learned fairly soon that it was the latter.

They rather hoped to get to the top so that they could get a better idea of the local geography than their walks had given them. Dar could see no sense in building a street that led to a mountain top, but was willing to suspend judgment until the evidence was in.

"In any case," the pilot pointed out, "if you really want to get up there, there's no need to follow a road. We've both climbed hills before."

"Yes, but I don't know about climbing this hill. Remember what happened over on the other side of town. It would be rather bad if another of those landslides started and we had no building to duck into."

"I don't think we need worry. The ground on this cone looks a lot firmer than that on the other, and I haven't seen any marks suggesting recent landslides."

"I didn't see any on the other side, either—and probably no one has been climbing this. Our disturbance might be all it was waiting for."

They might have spared themselves the discussion; they never reached the top. The road ceased to climb at about the time the last of the city except the submerged portion was lost to view, and without even discussing the question the two continued to follow the paved way. The view was already extensive; when they looked back the bottom of the harbor revealed the extent to which it must once have been dry land, as the street pattern of the city showed through the clear water. Ahead, the nearly straight coastline vanished in distance many miles away.

Inland, the jungle extended as far as the eye could reach. Even from this height—which was not, after all, very great—they could not begin to see across the distance separating them from the lava field where they had met. There seemed no reason, so far, for building the road at all; it seemed to lead nowhere. With mounting curiosity they hastened along it.

A quarter of a mile beyond the point where even the harbor had vanished from view they came upon the crater. There was virtually no warning; one moment the hillside sloped up and down away from the road at the usual angle; the next, the region downhill had vanished and the road was running perilously along the edge of a three-hundred-foot cliff. A heavy metal guard rail was there and the two approached this and leaned over.

The crater, if that was what it had once been, was not in the top of the hill, but well to one side; the road had led them to the highest point of its rim and the cone went up several hundred more feet behind them as they stood looking into it. It was not a very orthodox crater; the inner walls were sheer cliffs, which at first made Kruger feel decidedly insecure. Then he saw that the inner wall of the pit was not made of the same material as the hillside in general, and very slowly it dawned on him that the whole thing was artificial.

The walls were of concrete, or some equivalent composition. They had been shaped by tools. The bottom was not the tapering cone of the usual small crater but neither was it completely level. There was a small lake, and vegetation floored most of the rest of the area. Around the edge the concrete wall material seemed to extend horizontally for a short distance, and on this there was no vegetation. Both watchers were able to see the mouths of caves or tunnels opening from the wall onto this ramp, and with one mind they started looking for a way down.

There was nothing remotely resembling a ladder anywhere on the inner wall, so the logical thing to do seemed to be to follow the road, which must have been built in connection with this pit. This quickly gave promise of being the right course, as the path, instead of continuing around the mountain at the height which it had maintained for so long, began to curve downward in order to follow the rim of the pit. At the steepest part of the downhill slope the smooth surface of the pavement changed for about two hundred yards into something that might have been steps with very narrow treads and low risers or simply a corrugation to provide traction.

Shortly after this they reached a point where the trees grew right up to the edge of the road, overhanging both it and the pit. This had prevented their learning the course of the road from above; as it turned out, it had also prevented their seeing a number of buildings which were spaced at fairly regular intervals down the slope. These appeared to be built in the same style as the ones in the city except that they were all single-storied. Dar and Kruger wondered whether to examine them in detail now or find where the road led and come back later if there was time. The second alternative won.

However, it did not take long to find where the road led. Another two hundred yards down the slope it opened out into a paved space which Kruger labeled "parking lot" in his mind without even thinking. Several minutes of thought and investigation revealed no better name for it, so the two explorers returned to the buildings. Once inside the first of these, all recollection of the fact that they were already late for their appointment with the Teachers vanished from Kruger's mind.

His first supposition was that this must be the city power plant. An electric generator is going to look pretty much the same whoever builds it and whatever causes it to turn, and the objects in the first building were quite plainly electric generators. They were large, though Kruger lacked the knowledge to tell whether they were large enough to supply the whole city. Their great armatures were mounted on vertical axles, and apparently the source of mechanical energy was below ground level. With this in mind the two made a rapid search and were rewarded by finding the head of a ramp that led downward as expected.

The only difficulty was that the ramp was both narrow and low. Kruger would have to go down on his hands and knees, and the slope was steep. Even if he worked his way down backward return would be difficult if not impossible, for the ramp was floored with smooth metal and traction was very poor. Dar was in even worse case; the size question bothered him less, but his claws for the first time in the history of their acquaintance were less suited to the situation than Kruger's feet. Kruger finally decided that discretion was the better part of valor, and postponed exploration of the lower level until the other buildings had been examined.

This took some time, for the place was fascinating. All sorts of technical equipment were to be found. All of it was much too big to move, to Kruger's disappointment, but it left no doubt that the city builders were a highly civilized race. The generators and motors, furnaces and machine tools told all that was really important to know about them—except what had forced them to leave, to abandon their city and their equipment. War would have ruined both; plague should have left some traces of bodies, unless they were soft-bodied beings such as mollusks. Kruger, as a young man who had grown up on Earth during the first decade of interstellar exploration, was quite prepared to believe this last possibility, but even he did not take it for granted.

Always there were the conflicting facts: a partly submerged city which must have been abandoned for centuries—and machines with only a thin film of dust, pavings still free of vegetation, walls straight and uncracked with sound mortar and firm masonry which must have been maintained with care until fairly recently. It looked as though most of the machines would run if they were simply cleaned and power supplied to them.

The group of buildings, given time, would have served as a school in which any competent archaeologist could have learned practically anything which could be asked about their makers; one of them, in fact, might almost have been designed as a school. It contained a beautiful relief model of the two volcanoes, the city between, the harbor —though it did not show any water level—and the great pit beside which the building itself stood. In addition, many of the machines present full-scale in the other buildings were here in model form; the two investigators would probably have spent hours here alone had it not been for one fact.

70

There was another ramp leading downward from the single floor of this structure, and this time it was large enough for Dar to walk upright without difficulty. Also, its slope was much less than that of the preceding one, and the floor formed of a rough composition in which the little native's claws could readily find a grip. Finally, it led in toward the pit; and without further ado, once this fact was digested, the two started down its gentle slope.

The light was not good, but enough came from the building they had left to enable them to see any branches in the tunnel. For some time there was none; then a number of open doorways appeared on each side. Judging by echoes, they led into empty rooms; it was now too dark to check this by sight. A moment later, however, a faint light appeared ahead of them.

They did not turn all their attention on this light at once, however. Another distracting circumstance arose. At almost the same moment that Dar caught the illumination a whistling roar sounded behind them and they felt a sudden wave of heat. As one they leaped forward; and as they did so, sound and heat subsided. A faint draft from the building they had left carried a cloud of water vapor around them and on toward the end of the tunnel.

"What in the Pleiades was that?" Kruger asked of no one in particular.

"Another geyser?" Dar's response was only half a question.

"Awfully brief." Kruger started carefully back toward the source of the disturbance, ready to leap toward the pit once more if it seemed necessary.

It did. It happened again. And after some minutes of experiment it became evident that jets of live steam which played across the corridor were released by the weight of anyone standing or walking on the corridor floor approximately ten yards from the nozzles that supplied the steam.

"Which is interesting," Kruger concluded. "I suppose

71

we should be thankful that they set the thing up to warn us. It would have been just as easy, I should think, to put the trigger right in front of their blasted pipes."

"It would seem that they wanted to keep whatever was in here, inside," was Dar's contribution, "but didn't care if anyone or anything came in from outside. I find myself quite interested in what may be present at the other end of this tunnel. Do you have your knife, Nils?"

"I do. I'm right behind you, Robin Hood!"

With crossbow cocked and pointing forward the little Abyormenite strode down the slope toward the brightening light. Kruger followed. It occurred to both of them that the recent sounds would have destroyed any chance of taking whatever lay ahead by surprise, but neither mentioned this aloud.

VII. ENGINEERING

THEY NEEDN'T have worried. It was decidedly an anti-climax, but after more than an hour of searching the crater floor they were forced to conclude that there was no animal in the enclosure larger than a squirrel. This was a relief in one way, but left the reason for the trap in the tunnel even more obscure than it had been. They discussed this as they rested beside the pond and ate meat which Dar's bow had provided.

"Finding nothing living here is reasonable, I suppose, with the city deserted, but you'd think that there'd at least be a skeleton," Kruger remarked.

Dar scraped at the loamy soil with one claw.

"I don't know about that. Even bones from which flesh has been entirely eaten don't last very long, and if there's much meat left they go immediately. Still, you'd expect some traces of occupancy in those dens along the wall—the ones we saw from overhead." These openings had all been explored in search of either the inhabitant of the pit or another way out of it, but were nothing but concrete caves.

Kruger's tendency was to sit and theorize about the possible function of the crater in the days when the city was inhabited; Dar had a rather more practical question.

"Whether it was to keep bad people or bad animals means little to us just now," he said. "The trouble is it seems adequate to keep *us*, too. Admittedly, we will not starve; there is food and water. However, I have too few years to live to want to spend them in this place, and I am far from my books. Would it not be better to be planning a way out?"

"I suppose it would," Kruger admitted. "Still, if we

knew what was kept here we might have a better idea of how to do just that—if it was a lion cage and we knew it, we at least would know that the restraints were designed for lions. As it is—"

"As it is we know all about the restraints, as you call them. If we start up that tunnel it gets hot. I have no first-hand knowledge of what will happen if I walk into that steam, but I'm willing to assume that my Teachers had their reasons for keeping me away from such things. I notice that you, who are not afraid of fire, have shown no eagerness to get in front of those steam pipes either."

"True enough. I'm not afraid of fire that I control, but that doesn't apply here. But wait a minute—you said something just then. If we go up the tunnel we hit that trigger section of the floor, but that's not right in front of the jets. It can't extend very close to them, either, or we'd have been blistered on the way in. It should be possible to go up the corridor, get past the part of the floor that controls the valves, and wait there until the steam cuts off again, and then just walk out."

Dar was a little doubtful. "It seems too simple," he said. "What could they have been trying to hold here that would simply be scared of the noise? That's all that was really keeping it in, if your idea is right."

"Maybe that's just what it was," retorted Kruger. "Let's try it, anyway."

Neither of them was surprised this time when the roar of steam answered their weight on the significant floor section. Kruger led the way as close as he dared to the blast of hot gas, which emerged from nozzles at one side of the corridor and vanished—for the most part—into larger openings in the other. Bits of the streaming vapor eddied out of the line and curled about the two in swirling wisps of hot fog, but there was enough air to breathe, and for minute after minute they waited at the very edge of the jet of death.

At long last Kruger was forced to admit that Dar had been right. They were much closer to the steam than they had been when it first started on their way in, but it seemed that it was not going to stop now. Apparently the machinery was more complicated than Kruger had believed.

There was, of course, another possible interpretation. Kruger did not want to consider it. Whether or not it had occurred to Dar he did not know and carefully refrained from asking when they were back at the side of the pool.

"Do you suppose that the trap was for these little things we've been eating?" asked Dar after a long silence.

"Coming around to my logic?" queried Kruger. "I don't know, and don't see what good it will do us if it was."

"Neither did I until you spoke as you did a little while ago. However, I started to wonder just how much weight it took to set off that valve. We know that our combined weights will; I think that yours alone would, but we don't know whether mine would and if it did, how little could be placed on that part of the floor without starting the works."

"If yours touches it off what good would any further knowledge be?"

"It is not necessary to place all one's weight on one block, is it? It might be possible to place branches or logs on the floor so that we would—" Kruger was on his feet again; there was no need to finish the sentence. This time Dar led the way back up the tunnel, Kruger remaining several paces behind.

In due time the roar of steam showed that the trigger had been activated. Kruger stayed where he was, while Dar moved back toward him. The roar ceased; it was definitely Dar who had operated the valve. It was difficult to be sure of the precise position of the trigger block in the nearly dark passage. Dar moved back and forth until he had located the edge of the sensitive area to the last inch; then he spoke to his companion.

"Nils, if you will go back to the open space and find

some rocks of various weights we'll learn just how sensitive this thing is. I'll stay here and mark the place."

"Right." Kruger saw what the little fellow had in mind and obeyed without comment or question. He was back in five minutes with an armload of lava boulders whose total weight approximated Dar's fifty-five pounds, and the two proceeded to roll them one by one across the fatal line. Some minutes of alternate roaring and silence yielded evidence that the trigger was indeed operated by weight and that approximately fifteen pounds was required to open the valves. Further, the fifteen pounds could be applied at any point in the width of the corridor for a distance of at least ten feet. Merely spreading their weights would do no good, it seemed; as soon as the total reached the fifteen-pound limit the steam came on.

"We can still make a bridge right across the thing," pointed out Dar when this conclusion was reached.

"It's going to be a job," was Kruger's rather pessimistic reply. "Two knives will mean quite a lot of whittling."

"If you can think of something else I will be glad to try it. If not I suggest we start work." As was so often the case Dar's words seemed too sensible to oppose and they returned to the sunlight to seek materials.

Unfortunately, Kruger had been right too. They had the two knives, neither one particularly heavy. The trees of Abyormen differ among themselves as widely as those of any other planet, but none of them is soft enough to be felled with a sheath-knife in half an hour—or half a day. The travelers hoped to find something thick enough to carry them without bending noticeably and thin enough to cut and transport. The patch of forest in the crater was not very extensive, and they might have to be satisfied with much less than they wanted; neither could remember noticing a really ideal trunk during their earlier search, though of course they had had other matters in mind at the time.

Kruger was still dubious as they wandered about the

crater floor. He was no lazier than the average, but the thought of attacking even a six-inch trunk with his knife did not appeal to him. That situation has probably been responsible for most of the discoveries and inventions of the last half million years, so it is not too surprising that his mind was busy with other things as they hunted.

Nor is it surprising that some facts which had been available in the filing-case of his mind for some time should suddenly fall together; that seems to be the way ideas are usually born.

"Say, Dar," he said suddenly, "how come if this city is deserted, and the power plants presumably shut down, there is still all this steam? I can understand a simple lever-and-valve arrangement's lasting this long, but what about the energy supply?"

"There is much steam around," pointed out Dar. "Might they not have gone far underground, to tap the same fire that fed these volcanoes or the hot water at the village?" Kruger's face fell a little, as he realized he should have thought of this himself.

"Just the same," he said, "it seems to me that there can be only so much steam there. Why shouldn't we leave some rocks on that trigger and just wait for the thing to run out?"

"It's been running, on and off, for quite a while now," said Dar doubtfully, "and hasn't shown any signs of running down. Still, I suppose there's a chance. Anyway, once the weight is in place it won't use any of our time; we can go back to this job. Let's do it."

"It won't take both of us. I'll be right back." Kruger returned to the tunnel, rolled one of the rocks they had left on the floor toward the trap until his ears told him it had gone far enough, and was back with Dar in less than two minutes.

By the perversity of fortune the only tree that seemed usable for their purpose was located about as far from the tunnel as it could be. Complaining about it would do no good, however, and the two set to work with their tiny blades. Its wood was softer than pine, but even so the seven-inch trunk took some time to cut through in the circumstances. They rested several times, and stopped to hunt and eat once, before the big plant came down.

This particular tree arranged its branches in more or less the fashion of a multi-layered umbrella, with four or five feet between layers. The plan was to save some of the branches from the layer nearest the base and from that nearest the top, so that they could serve as "legs" to keep the weight of the main trunk and its burdens off the ground. Kruger would not have been too surprised had the job taken a year, but determination and increasing skill paid their dividends and only a few terrestrial days passed before the work was ready to be dragged to the tunnel. Throughout that time the howl of the steam never subsided; there was no need to visit the tunnel to check the jets' behavior. If there was any diminution in the sound it was too gradual for either of them to detect while they worked; the phenomenon that did attract their attention was its sudden stopping.

This happened just as they were starting to drag the log toward the tunnel. For a moment the echoes of the whistling roar played back and forth across the pit; then silence took their place. Dar and Kruger looked at each other for a moment, then, without pausing for discussion, started running toward the opening.

Dar reached it first in spite of his shorter legs; the undergrowth barring the way was sufficiently open to let him through fairly easily while Kruger had to force his way. The floor of the tunnel was wet with a trickle of near-boiling water, evidently from steam which had condensed on the walls and roof during the past few dozen hours. The air in the passage was only saved from being unbreathable by the draft entering it from the pit; only a few yards of the corridor could be seen in the swirling fog. Step by step they advanced as the current drove the mist curtain before it, and presently they reached the stones that had been left near the trigger block. Dar would have continued, but Kruger restrained him with a word of caution.

"Let's hold it a moment and see whether the rock I put on the trigger is still there. Maybe it got washed off by the stream; it wasn't very heavy." Dar privately felt that a fifteen-pound boulder would need something more powerful than the trickle in the tunnel to shift it, but stopped anyway. Only a few moments were needed to see that the rock was still in place; presumably the trigger was still depressed, and therefore the steam had been shut off by some other cause. A little uneasily, Kruger shifted his own weight forward until he was beside the rock. Nothing happened, and for several seconds the two looked thoughtfully at each other. The same possibilities were passing through their minds.

Neither knew the details of the valve system that controlled the steam. There might be any number of safety devices for shutting it off before complete exhaustion of the supply—devices which could be overridden by other triggers if a determined effort was made to escape through the corridor. The trouble was that the makers were not human and, as far as could be told, not members of Dar's race either; there was simply no way of guessing what they might have considered logical design.

"I guess there's only one way to find out, Dar. You'd better let me go first; I could probably stand a brief dose if the thing started up, but from what your Teachers have said there's no telling what it would do to you."

"That's true, but my weight is less. Perhaps it would be better if I were to start."

"What good will that do? If it doesn't trip for you we still won't know that it won't for me. You just be set to come on the double if I make it." Dar offered no further argument but helped his big companion make sure that the small amount of equipment he carried was securely fastened—neither one wanted to come back for

79

anything that was dropped. With this accomplished Kruger wasted no more time; he set off up the tunnel as fast as his strength would allow.

Dar watched until he was sure that the boy was well past the steam jets; then he followed. He caught up with Kruger at the mouth of the tunnel, but the two did not stop until they were outside the building from which the passage led. No sound had come from behind them, and gradually Kruger's panting slowed as he waited and listened.

"I guess that did it," he said at last. "Now what do we do? We're something like half a year late for our talk with that Teacher back at the village; do you think we can persuade him that our lateness was accidental, and that he'll be in a mood to give back your books?"

Dar thought for some time. Even he had become a little tired of being put off each time he asked for his property, and Kruger's implied point was a good one. Dar was fair-minded enough to admit to himself that their lateness was not entirely accidental; they should have started back to the village well before the time they became trapped in the crater.

"I wonder why the villagers did not come after us?" he asked suddenly. "They knew about where we were and they certainly were able to find us the other time."

"That's a good question and I can't see any answer offhand. The steam shouldn't have scared them away; they were used to those geysers."

"Do you suppose they could have known we were trapped and been satisfied to leave us where we were? A searching party could have heard the steam from a long distance and checked up on us by simply looking over the crater edge."

"That's a distinct possibility—except that the trap was so easy to get out of that they would hardly suppose we could be permanently held by it. In that case there would still be guards around, and they'd probably have met us on the way out."

"Perhaps there was only a single guard, who didn't think the noise would lead to anything—they might think of the jet as inexhaustible; I'm sure I would have. In that case he might only have just started for reinforcements. I'm armed, and he might not feel it his duty to attempt our capture single-handed."

"A possibility which we have no means of checking—except by waiting here to see whether the soldiers turn out. Should we do that?"

"I—guess not." Dar was still a little reluctant in his answer. "You were probably right all along. We have been wasting time and I have only sixteen years. We had better start for the Ice Ramparts once more and hope we can get there in time to return here with enough aid to get the books."

"That suits me—it always has. This steam bath gets no more comfortable with time; in fact, I'd swear it got a little hotter each year. Let's go—and fast." They suited action to the word and left mountain and city behind them without further discussion.

Travel was a little easier along the seacoast. The beach was usually of hard-packed sand, though it was almost always narrow—Abyormen had no moon massive enough to raise noticeable tides, and this close to the pole even those caused by Theer were not enough to measure. Kruger had been a little doubtful about their traveling on a surface that took their tracks so clearly, but Dar pointed out that they had told enough since their capture to give any would-be pursuers the proper direction. Speed, and speed alone, was all that would serve the fugitives at this point.

There were numerous animals in the forest, which came unbroken to the beach, and none of them seemed to have any particular fear of the travelers. Time and again Dar's crossbow knocked over their dinner, which was dissected on the spot and eaten either as they traveled or during the occasional stops which were needed for sleep.

81

Once or twice the tips of volcanic cones could be seen well inland, but only once did one of them hamper their travel in any way. Then they had to spend some hours working their way across a small field of lava which had flowed into the sea at some time in the past.

Usually they could see the coast for miles behind them, and oftener than not one of Dar's eyes was turned in that direction, but the only moving things he ever saw were wild animals, usually quite unconcerned with the travelers.

The trip became a monotony of walking in steaming heat or unpleasantly warm rain. Occasionally Kruger interrupted the traveling with a bath in the sea; warm though the water was, the refreshment resulting from the swim made him feel the risk was worth while. He did this only when Dar wanted to rest, since the Abyormenite had no use for swimming and seemed to think of little except the amount of time they were spending en route.

They had no precise means of measuring the distance they traveled, so that not even Dar could guess when the islands they were seeking would appear; but appear they eventually did. Dar gave a grunt of relief when the first of the little humps appeared far out on the horizon.

"Fifteen years to go. We'll make it yet." His confidence may have been a trifle misplaced, but Kruger's ignorance of the scale of the maps he had seen kept him from realizing that the island chain by which Dar meant to proceed led across eight hundred miles of ocean, and that almost as much land lay between its end and the point on the ice cap which was their goal. He assumed the native's judgment to be sound and almost relaxed.

"How do we get across the sea?" he contented himself with asking.

"We float." And Dar Lang Ahn meant it.

This worried Kruger, and his worry did not grow less as time went on. It became increasingly evident that Dar intended to make his trip on a raft, which was the only sort of craft their tools would allow them to build; and even his ignorance of the distance to be covered did not make the boy any happier at the prospect. There was no provision being made for sails; when Kruger mentioned this and finally managed to explain what sails were the pilot explained that the wind always blew against them anyway. They would have to paddle.

"Does the wind *never* change?" Kruger asked in dismay as he considered the task of moving by muscle power the unwieldy thing that was beginning to take shape on the beach.

"Not enough to matter."

"But how do you know?"

"I have been flying this route all my life, and a glider cannot be flown by one who does not know what the currents are doing."

"Didn't you say that this island chain marked the air route your gliders always take to the Ice Ramparts?" Kruger asked suddenly.

"Those coming from Kwarr, yes."

"Then why haven't we seen any?"

"You have not been looking up. I have seen three since we reached this spot. If your eyes were only on the sides of your head and stuck out a little more—"

"Never mind my optical deficiencies! Why didn't you signal them?"

"How?"

"You were going to reflect sunlight from your belt buckles when I found you; or we could light a fire."

"Your fire-lighter is in the keeping of our friends whom we have left behind, and even if we lighted one you should know by now that one of my people would not approach a fire. If the pilot saw the smoke he would avoid it and more than likely report it as a new center of volcanic activity."

"But how about the reflection? Your buckles are still shiny!"

"How does one aim a beam of light from a mirror?

83

I was using the method when you found me because it was the only possible one; I would have been as dead, had you not appeared, as I shall be less than fifteen years from now."

"Can't you see the beam of light that the buckle reflects?"

"No. I once saw a mirror so perfectly flat that one could see the ray of sunlight coming from it if there were a little haze in the air, but my buckles are not in that class."

"Then if they spread the beam it should be that much easier to hit something with it. Why do you not try, at least?"

"I think it would be a waste of time, but if you can suggest a way of pointing the beam reasonably closely you may try the next time a glider comes in sight."

"Let me see the buckles, please."

Dar complied with the air of one amusing a rather dull child. Kruger examined the plates of metal carefully. They were more nearly flat than Dar's words had led him to hope, rectangular in shape, about two inches wide and four long. Two holes about an inch square were present in each one, and between these a single small circular hole which in service held a peg for securing the leather straps threaded through the larger openings. Kruger smiled as he finished his examination, but handed them back to their owner without any comment except, "I'll take you up on that offer. Let me know when another glider appears, if I don't see it myself."

Dar went back to work with little interest in Kruger's idea, whatever it might be, but he obediently kept one eye roving about the horizon. He was a little annoyed that Kruger was now constantly lifting his head to do the same thing, but was fair-minded enough to admit that the poor creature couldn't help it. He was even more annoyed when Kruger proved the first to spot an approaching aircraft, but watched with interest as the boy prepared to use the buckles in signaling.

All he saw, however, was that a buckle was held before one of the small eyes, which apparently sighted through the center hole at the approaching glider. Dar could see no reason why this should give any assistance in aiming the reflected beam. He did see the spot of light shining through the same central opening on Kruger's face, but had no means of telling that the boy had so placed the mirror that the reflection of his own features in its back had taken a definite position—one which brought the spot of sunlight on the reflected face directly on the hole through which he was looking at the glider. Holding himself as motionless as possible, he spoke.

"Do you have any special signal that depends on flashes of light—something the pilot would definitely recognize?"

"No."

"Then we'll just have to hope that he'll be curious about a constant blink." Kruger began rocking the mirror back and forth as he spoke.

Dar Lang Ahn was astonished when the actions of the aircraft showed plainly that its occupant had seen the flashes and he made no secret of the fact. Kruger passed it off as an everyday occurrence. He was still young, after all.

VIII. TRANSPORTATION

THE GLIDER did not land; its pilot was too cautious for that. Whatever might be making the flashes on the beach below was almost certainly not a launching catapult and if he touched the ground he would stay there. He had books of his own and had no intention of risking them. Nevertheless he skimmed low enough to make out the figures of Dar and Kruger and to be as puzzled by the latter as Dar had been.

One advantage of a glider is its silence. This characteristic, combined with the hyper-acute hearing of the Abyormenites, enabled a conversation to take place between Dar and the glider pilot. It was carried out in snatches as the aircraft swooped over and interrupted until it had passed on, turned into the updraft at the edge of the forest, picked up the altitude it had lost, and returned for another pass. Eventually, however, Dar got across the fact which he considered most important —the whereabouts of his books.

"I understand," the pilot called down at length. "I will go on, turn in my load, and give your report. You had better stay where you are. Is there anything else that should be known by the Teachers?"

"Yes. My companion. You can see he is not a person. He knows much that is not in the books; he should go to the Teachers himself."

"Does he speak?"

"Yes, though not well. He has words of his own, which are different from ours, and has not learned all ours yet."

"Do you know any of his?"

"Some, yes."

"Then perhaps it would be best if we brought you

along, too. It will save time and there is not too much more of that."

"I am not sure, but I get the impression that he does not die at the proper time; he expects to live longer. There may be no need of haste."

One of the frequent interruptions to regain altitude allowed this information to sink into the pilot's mind. When he swung past again:

"In any case remain with him. I will report all you have told me and someone will return to give you the decision of the Teachers. If you could improvise a catapult capable of launching a four-man glider it might expedite matters, since the portable ones are probably dismantled by now." He passed on and began to circle in determined fashion for altitude, while Dar turned to Kruger to answer his questions about the numerous parts of the conversation the boy had either not heard or not understood.

"I had suspected, but found it hard to believe," Kruger said at the end.

"What?"

"That this 'time' you have mentioned so often means the end of your life. How can it be that you know when you are going to die?"

"I have known it all my life; it is part of the knowledge in the books. Life starts, and continues for a measured time, and ends. That is why the books must go to the Ice Ramparts, so that the Teachers may use them to help instruct the people who come after."

"You mean everyone dies at the same time?"

"Of course. Practically all lives started at the same time—except the few who have had accidents and had to start over."

"How do you die?"

"We do not know, though the Teachers may. They have always told us the time but never the manner."

"What sort of people are these Teachers?"

"Why, they are not people. They are—they are

Teachers. That is, they look like people but are much bigger—bigger even than you."

"Do they look more like your people than I do, or are there other differences like those between you and me?"

"They are exactly like me except for size—and the fact that they know so much, of course."

"And they live on from one generation to the next—that is, through the time of one group of people and into that of the next—while all ordinary people die when the time comes?"

"So they, and the books, say."

"How long is the time that you normally live?"

"Eight hundred and thirty years. We are now in the eight hundred and sixteenth." Kruger thought this over and did a little mental arithmetic, and tried to imagine how he would feel knowing that he had just under nine months to live. He knew it would bother him; Dar Lang Ahn seemed to take it as a matter of course. Kruger could not help wondering whether his little friend had any secret wishes concerned with a longer life span. He did not quite dare ask; it seemed to have the possibility of being a very touchy subject. He allowed the conversation to drift in the direction Dar was leading it. The little pilot seemed actually to pity him, Kruger finally realized, for *not* knowing when his own life was due to end; while he did not have the precise words to express his feelings, and they were a little too abstract to explain clearly, the boy got a definite impression that Dar considered the suspense of such a situation to be something he would not care to face.

"But enough of that." Dar, too, seemed to feel that he was verging on what might prove an uncomfortable subject for his companion. "The pilot suggested that we try to set up a catapult so that they can take you off. We should at least be able to get it started before they come back. All we really need is the stakes; they will certainly bring the cables when they come."

"How does the catapult work?"

Dar gave an explanation. Apparently it was simply an overgrown slingshot. The complication in its construction lay first in the need for placing it so that it could hurl the glider into a reasonably dependable updraft, and second in making sure that the supporting structure to which the cable was hooked could stand the strain—a flimsily assembled mass of timber suddenly coming loose and snapping back toward the glider could be decidedly embarrassing. The first requirement was not difficult to satisfy on the seashore; the second was a matter of experience. The work was actually easier than the raft building had been, since the pieces of wood used were much thinner. Kruger cut most of them with his knife to Dar's specifications; the little native placed them and propped them with speed and skill.

Arren, circling lazily above the horizon, marked the passage of time, but neither workman noticed it particularly. They stopped to hunt and eat or for necessary rest, but Kruger never knew just how long it took the glider they had seen to complete its journey to the ice cap, and for the relief expedition to be organized and make the return. It was certainly less than a year—they never saw Theer at all between the two events—but when the first of the gliders skimmed in from over the sea the catapult was ready.

The machine settled reasonably close to the catapult. Two others followed it within the next half hour, and a single pilot climbed from each. Dar performed the introductions; all three were acquaintances of his. Neither then nor later was Kruger able to tell them apart, and he was embarrassed to find that he could not distinguish Dar from the others except by familiar stains, nicks, and scratches on his friend's leather harness and the iron buckles he had used for signaling. The others had bits of metal about them, but not serving the same functions; their harness buckles appeared to be of something like horn.

Their names were Dar En Vay, Ree San Soh, and Dar Too Ken. Kruger was bothered by the multiplicity of Dars, realizing that he could no longer indulge his habit of shortening his friend's name for convenience. He wondered if the names connoted any sort of family connection—though from what Dar Lang Ahn had been telling him that seemed unlikely.

One of the gliders was considerably larger than the other two; Kruger supposed it was the "four-man" machine the other pilot had mentioned. Dar Lang Ahn called him over to it and the whole party went into consultation as to the best way of accommodating the relatively huge human body. The control seat, of course, had to be left in place for the pilot; if the three others were simply removed it left nothing to support Kruger except the frail envelope of the fuselage. No one of the seats was large enough to hold him, of course, though they were quite reasonably shaped from the human point of view. The final solution was an improvised support of slender branches, more like a mattress than a seat, which appeared to be strong enough to keep Kruger from going through to the fabric and light enough to meet the rather exacting balance requirements of the glider—requirements which were already being strained a trifle by the boy's physical characteristics.

Kruger gathered that some time elapsed between the dying off of one race and the appearance of the next, but when he put the question to the group no one was able to answer him. The three newcomers were startled at the question and from then on seemed to regard him as more of a freak than even his admittedly strange appearance warranted. The pilot of the large glider made no objection when it was suggested that Dar Lang Ahn fly it as long as Kruger was aboard.

With this arrangement completed Dar asked where the rest of the fleet might be, or whether a group this size was expected to raid the village where his books were held. Ree San Soh answered him.

"We are not going to that village yet. The Teachers wanted to get a more complete report on the situation, which could only be obtained from you, and they also want to see your companion Kruger. You said that he knew more than was in the books, so they feel that it is more important to get him to the Ice Ramparts, particularly if he suffers from heat."

Dar Lang Ahn admitted the force of this reasoning, although a lifetime of habit prevented his being completely easy on the subject of his lost cargo. Kruger applauded the decision; every time he heard the word which he had decided must mean "ice," he felt homesick. A Turkish bath is all right now and then, but he had been in one for the best part of a terrestrial year.

There was no difficulty with the launching. Each glider in turn was anchored at the proper distance, the cable hooked to its nose, and a light, non-stretching line run up to the bracket, through a pulley, and back to a capstan. The latter was wound up until the stretching portion of the line reached the bracket, then the first line was detached and stowed and the glider was released. As it lunged forward over the bracket the hook disengaged from its nose and fell free, leaving the performance to be repeated with the next glider.

The only variation was with the last aircraft, which was the one used by Dar Lang Ahn and Kruger. In this case the detachable hook was fastened to the bracket instead of the craft, the capstan was installed on a support in the cockpit, and the glider was anchored by a slip knot that could be released by the pilot from his station. As a result the cable rode into the air along with them and was wound up by Kruger when they were safely airborne. Not until after this was finished did Dar comment on the consequences which would have ensued had the hook fouled in the launching bracket.

"But don't you have some means of releasing this end of the cable if that happens?" asked Kruger.

"It's been tried but usually the pilot doesn't react fast

enough to get any good out of it. You don't know it's fouled until the cable jerks your nose down and breaks you out of your safety belt." Kruger gulped and was silent.

The flight was interesting but relatively uneventful. It was slow, of course, by Kruger's standards; Dar could scarcely ever head straight toward an objective. He had to coast from one rising air current to the next and Kruger was by no means always sure just how he found his updrafts. Dar, of course, could not always explain his knowledge; it had taken him a lifetime of about forty terrestrial years to pick it up and he could hardly impart it all in one flight.

One thing was certain: Dar Lang Ahn could have walked away with any sailplane prize ever offered on Earth without even realizing that he had been in a competition. The mere fact that the present flight covered over fifteen hundred miles was not the principal reason for this; rather it was the fact that he should take such a flight as a matter of course, with no more concern about the possibility of failure than a man considers when he starts to drive from Honolulu to New York. As the hours passed with no sign of the further shore Kruger began gradually to appreciate some of this.

When the coast finally did appear it was totally different in nature from the one they had left. That had been relatively flat, except for occasional volcanic cones; this was rugged. There were ranges of mountains produced quite obviously by both thrusting and block faulting—apparently young mountains, as geologists class such things. Steep cliffs, thousands of tiny streams rich in waterfalls and rapids, sharp, bare peaks—all told the same story. The air currents were incredibly complex and Dar used them with a skill bordering on the supernatural. The other gliders had long since disappeared; their lower wing loadings had enabled them to make "jumps" from updraft to updraft which Dar had not been willing to risk.

With the coast in sight Dar had begun to work to the left, and crossed it on a long slant. Usually they were too high for any animals to be seen or even the details of the forests that clothed the lower slopes of the mountains, but sometimes the glider would drift along the leeward side of a valley to make use of the air currents being forced up the next ridge, and Kruger could see that the trees were different. One reason was fairly evident: the temperature was lower, as Kruger could easily feel. At the highest altitudes reached by the glider he had felt comfortable at the start of the flight, now the comfort point was much closer to the ground.

This grew worse as the hours passed. Kruger was not sure how far they traveled but realized that it must be hundreds of miles. He was tired, hungry, and thirsty. Dar seemed indifferent to all these ills, as well as to the cold which was beginning to make his human companion almost regret the jungle. They had spoken little for many hours but each time Kruger thought of asking how much longer the flight was to last he was stopped by his reluctance to appear complaining. Eventually it was Dar who spoke.

"We may not make it before dark," he said suddenly. "I'll have to land soon, and go on when the sun comes up again." Kruger looked in surprise at the blue star, whose motions he had long since ceased to notice particularly. Dar was right, it seemed. Arren was almost on the horizon behind them and a little to the glider's right; it was very slowly going down. Kruger tried to use this fact to form an idea of his location on the planet—it must mean something, since he had seen the blue sun in the sky constantly for over six terrestrial months. One point seemed clear: Theer would not rise this year. They had crossed to the "dark side" of Abyormen. An ice cap suddenly seemed a reasonable feature of the landscape.

Nevertheless, judging by the angle at which the star was setting it should not go very far below the horizon, Kruger decided. He put this point to Dar.

"It will not actually get too dark to see, will it?" he asked.

"No, but we do not habitually fly when neither sun is in the sky," was the answer. "Vertical air currents are much rarer and harder to identify from any distance. However, I will do my best to get to the Ramparts before the sun goes down; I have no great appetite for sitting on a hilltop for fifteen or twenty hours." Kruger concurred heartily in this wish.

It was hard to tell just what the star was doing, since their altitude varied so widely and rapidly, but that it was setting there could be no doubt. His attention was so concentrated on the vanishing star that he failed to note the landscape below as he might otherwise have done, and the ice cap was in sight for some time before he noticed it. After that he noticed little else.

A great river flowing under their course toward the now distant sea was the first warning that caught his eye. Following it upstream he saw that it rose at the foot of a gigantic wall that gleamed pinkly in the nearly level rays of Alcyone. It took him several seconds to realized that the wall was the foot of a glacier. The river continued inland, but it was a river of ice. The mountains actually were higher toward the center of the continent, but to Kruger's view now they seemed to shrink, for their bases were buried in what looked like the accumulated snows of centuries. As far as the eye could reach from the highest point of the glider's flight the field of ice spread on. Most of it was held motionless by the great hills that strove to pierce it from beneath, but near the edge the glaciers oozed free and tried to make their way to the ocean. The ice was certainly a thousand feet or more thick here at the edge of the cap; Kruger wondered what it could be further inland.

But the sight of the ice cap meant that they could not be far from their goal; Dar would not have come so close to a fruitful source of downdrafts unless he had to. The pilot admitted this when Kruger asked him. "We should make it, all right. About two more climbs, if I can find good enough updrafts, and we can coast the rest of the way." The boy forbore to interrupt him any more and watched the landscape in fascination as forest gave way to patches of snow and ice, and soil to black and gray rock streaked with white.

Eventually the pilot pointed, and following his finger the boy saw what could only be their landing place. It was a level platform, apparently a natural terrace, far up the side of one of the mountains. The valley below was filled with ice, part of a glacier which remained solid for fully a dozen more miles after flowing beneath this point. The terrace was simply an entryway; the mouths of several huge tunnels which seemed to lead deep into the mountain were visible opening onto it. Several winged shapes lying near the tunnel mouths left no doubt of the nature of the place.

To Kruger it seemed as though they could glide to it from their present position, but Dar Lang Ahn knew only too well the fierce downdrafts present along the edge of the terrace when the sun was not shining on the mountain face, and took his last opportunity to climb. For two or three minutes as he circled, the glider was in the last rays of Alcyone and must have been visible to the watchers on the terrace below.

Then the star vanished behind a peak and the terrace swelled under the aircraft's nose. Dar brought the machine across the level space with five hundred feet to spare, made two tight slipping turns within its confines to get rid of the excess altitude, and settled like a feather in front of one of the tunnel openings. Kruger, half-frozen from the last climb, stumbled thankfully out of the machine and gratefully accepted the water jug which one of the waiting natives immediately presented him.

Apparently they were expected—naturally enough; the other gliders must have arrived long before.

"Do you need rest before talking to the Teachers?" asked one of those who had met them. Dar Lang Ahn looked at Kruger, who he knew had been awake much longer than he normally was, but to his surprise the boy answered, "No; let's go. I can rest later; I'd like to see your Teachers and I know Dar Lang Ahn is in a hurry to get back to the village. Is it far to their office?"

"Not very distant." Their questioner led the way back into the tunnel, which presently turned into a spiral ramp leading downward. They followed it for what seemed fully half an hour to the boy, who began to wonder just what their guide considered "very distant," but finally the slope eased off onto the level floor of a large cavern. The cave itself was nearly deserted, but several doors led into it, and their guide headed them toward one of these.

The room beyond proved to be an office and was occupied by two beings who were rather obviously, from Dar Lang Ahn's description, Teachers. As he had said, they were identical with him in appearance, with the single exception of their size. These creatures were fully eight feet tall.

They each took a step toward the newcomers and waited silently for introductions. Their motions were slow and a trifle clumsy, Kruger noted, and with that observation the suspicion he had entertained for some time grew abruptly in his mind to a virtual certainty.

IX. TACTICS

EARTH LIES some five hundred light years from Alcyone and the star cluster in which it lies. This is not far as galactic distances go, so it must have been some time before Nils Kruger first met Dar Lang Ahn that the data gathered by the *Alphard* was delivered to the home planet. Since the survey vessel had obtained spectra, photometric and stereometric readings, and physical samples from some five hundred points in the space occupied by the Pleiades as well as biological and meteorological data from about a dozen planets within the cluster, there was a good deal of observational matter to be reduced.

In spite of this, the planet where Nils Kruger was presumed to have died came in for attention very quickly. There was not enough data on hand to make known its orbit about the red dwarf sun to which it was presumably attached or the latter's relationship to the nearby Alcyone, but a planet, a dwarf sun, and a giant sun all close together within a mass of nebular gas form together a situation which is rather peculiar by most of the cosmological theories. The astrophysicist who first came across the material looked at it again, then called a colleague; announcement cards went out, and a burning desire to know more began to be felt among the ranks of the astronomers. Nils Kruger was not quite as dead as he himself believed.

But Kruger himself was not an astronomer, and while he had by now a pretty good idea of the sort of orbit Abyormen pursued about its sun he knew no reason to suppose that the system should be of special interest to anyone but himself. He had put thoughts of Earth out of his mind—almost, for he had something else to consider. He expected to live out his life on Abyormen; he had found only one being there whom he considered a personal friend. Now he had been informed by the friend himself that their acquaintance could last only a few more of Kruger's months, that the other would die his natural death at the end of that time.

Kruger didn't believe it or, at least, didn't believe it was necessary. Dar Lang Ahn's description of the Teachers had aroused a suspicion in his mind. His sight of the great creatures had confirmed those suspicions, and he settled down to his first conversation with them possessed of a grim determination to do everything in his power to postpone the end that Dar Lang Ahn regarded as inevitable. It did not occur to him to question whether or not he would be doing a favor to Dar Lang Ahn in the process.

There is no way of telling whether the Teachers who questioned Nils Kruger sensed his underlying hostility to them; no one asked them during the short remainder of their lives, and they did not bother to record mere suspicions. They certainly showed none themselves; they were courteous, according to their standards, and answered nearly as many questions as they asked. They showed no surprise at the astronomical facts Kruger was forced to mention in describing his background; they asked many of the same questions that the Teacher of the villagers had put to him earlier. He pointed out that the previous Teacher had kept his fire-lighter, when the conversation went that way; he was prepared to defend Dar Lang Ahn's association with fire, but the Teachers did not seem bothered by the fact. Dar's relief at this was evident even to Kruger.

The Teachers showed him the Ice Ramparts in considerable detail—more than Dar Lang Ahn himself had ever seen. The caverns in the mountain were only an outpost; the main settlement was far underground and miles further inland. Several tunnels connected it with landing stages similar to the one on which they had arrived. It was here that the libraries were located; they saw load after load of the books which had come in from the cities scattered over Abyormen being filed for further distribution. Asked when this would take place the Teacher made no bones about the answer.

"It will be about four hundred years after the end of this life until the next starts. Within ten years after that the cities should be peopled again and the process of educating the populations begin."

"Then you have already started to abandon your cities. Do all your people come here to die?"

"No. We do not abandon our cities; the people live in them to the end."

"But the one Dar Lang Ahn and I found was abandoned!"

"That was not one of our cities. The people who lived near it were not our people and their Teachers were not of our kind."

"Did you know about this city?"

"Not exactly, though those Teachers are not complete strangers to us. We are still undecided about what to do in that connection." Dar interrupted here.

"We'll simply have to go back with enough people to take the books away—and I'm sure you want Nils's fire-lighter, too, even though we don't use fire. It is knowledge and should go into the libraries."

The Teacher made the affirmative hand motion.

"You are quite right, up to a point. However, it is more than doubtful that we could force the return of the material. Did you not say that the books had been taken into a shelter among the hot-water pools?"

"Yes, but—they can't have been kept there!"

"I am less sure than you. In any case if we made an attack as you suggest they would have the time, and probably the inclination, to hide the things elsewhere."

"But couldn't we make them tell where?" asked Kruger. "Once we captured the place it could be a simple bargain —their lives for our property."

The Teacher looked steadily at the boy for a moment, using both eyes.

"I don't think I could approve of taking their lives," he said at last. Kruger felt a little uncomfortable under the steady stare.

"Well—they needn't know that we wouldn't actually do it," he pointed out rather lamely.

"But suppose their Teachers still have the things? What good will threatening the people do?"

"Won't we have the Teachers too?"

"I doubt it." The dryness of the answer escaped Kruger completely.

"Well even if we don't, don't they care enough about their people to give up the things in order to save them?"

"That might be." The Teacher paused. "That might—very—well—be. I am rendered a little uncomfortable by some of your ideas, but I must confess there are germs of value in that one. We need not threaten to kill, either; simply removing the people would be enough—or rather, threatening to do it. I must discuss this with the others. You may stay and examine the library if you wish, but I imagine you will want to be back at the outpost when a decision is reached."

Kruger had seen all he wanted of the book-storing process and of the librarians, who were people of Dar's stature rather than Teachers, so he signified his intention of returning to the surface. Dar Lang Ahn came along and the long walk up the tunnel commenced. It was enough to keep Kruger warm, though the temperature was about forty-five Fahrenheit. He wondered as they traveled at the need for such a shelter—there was half a mile of rock and over three miles of ice overhead, according to the Teacher. Even more remarkable was the construction of such a place by people whose tools seemed to be of the simplest. But no doubt they had had tools when they first came; Kruger now believed that the accident which had marooned Dar's people on Abyormen must have occurred several generations before. For one thing there was obviously more than one shipload of them on the planet.

The discussion of Kruger's projects and its modification by the Teachers took quite some time, and the boy spent the interval seeing what he could do both inside the station and out.

The temperature outside was just about freezing, as might have been expected with so much ice in the vicinity. Kruger could not stay out for very long at a time, since his coveralls had been improvised with the thought in mind of keeping him cool. Fortunately the synthetic of which they were made was windproof, and by tightening the wrists, ankles, and neck he was able to gain some protection. Dar Lang Ahn, who accompanied him on most of his trips outside, seemed indifferent to the cold as he had been to the heat.

On one occasion Kruger did remain outside for a long time, but it was quite involuntary. He had gone out alone, and after plowing through drifts and over treacherous crust for half an hour or so had returned to find the door locked. He had not checked it on leaving to find what sort of latch it had, and apparently it was a spring lock. No amount of pounding attracted anyone's attention, since the door was a quarter of a mile from the main cavern on that level, and at last Kruger had to strike off around the mountain to the landing platform. He reached it more dead than alive, and thereafter was quite careful about doors.

Even inside he occasionally made mistakes, as well. Once he nearly suffocated in a food-storage bin he was examining, and on another occasion came within an ace of dropping through what later proved to be the trap of a rubbish-disposal chute. He learned later that the chute led to a narrow canyon full of melt-water which normally carried away the rubbish. Thereafter he went nowhere alone. He was decidedly relieved when the deliberations ended and the plan of attack was decided.

It was reasonably ingenious, he felt. He and Dar were

to return to the city by glider, circling over the village to be sure they were seen. In the meantime a large force of bowmen were to land on the other side, far enough from the city to be assured of secrecy, and enter it. The two groups were to meet at a point which Dar selected, drawing a map with the aid of his photographic memory and marking the position on it.

The assumption was that the villagers would once more send a force to capture the intruders. This group would be led into a square by Dar and Kruger, which was surrounded by buildings in which the bowmen from the ice cap would be sheltered. There was the possibility that the two decoys would be held as hostages or even killed out of hand, but Dar did not appear worried and Kruger therefore preferred not to show his own feelings.

Kruger made sure that food and water were stowed in the big glider this time, though Dar appeared to consider them unnecessary for such a trip.

The return to the tropics, of course, pleased Kruger only briefly. After a very short time in the steamy air on the wrong side of the ocean he found himself thinking wistfully of the winds from the ice cap—quite humanly ignoring the fact that those winds had nearly been the death of him on one occasion. It is hard to imagine just how Dar Lang Ahn would have reacted had he known his companion's thoughts. Since Kruger kept them carefully to himself the pilot was able to concentrate on his business.

The volcanic cones were found without difficulty. Most of the other gliders were already down on the beach a few miles short of the mountains; as before, the lighter craft had made better time. Dar and Kruger could see the crews below them gathering for the trip to the city and decided to remain airborne for a while longer to make sure that the bowmen would have time to get into position.

They went on up the coast beyond the cones and cast about in an attempt to find the village of their captors from the air.

The huts themselves were too well concealed by the trees, it turned out, but the area of the geysers was easy enough to locate. The heat from this region provided a splendid updraft and Dar circled in it for several minutes while the two examined the area minutely, but there was no sign of life now. At length Dar took his glider back to the volcanoes and landed on the beach as close as he could get to the city.

They entered the place on foot, fully aware that they were leaving a plain trail in the sand of the beach but not worried about it. At least, Dar Lang Ahn was not worried; Kruger was beginning to wonder whether or not they might be getting just a little too blatant about the whole business. He suggested this to his companion, to whom the idea was wholly new.

"I don't think we need worry too much," Dar said at length. "They will see that we had to land on the beach; we certainly could not bring the glider down in the jungle, and there is no way of walking across sand without leaving a trail. We can be less obvious inside the city."

"All right." Kruger was coming to suspect that Dar Lang Ahn's people had had little practice in military matters. However, with luck, the villagers they sought to trap might prove equally naive; there was nothing much that could be done about it at this point.

The city lay silent, as it had before. There had been a recent rainstorm, and puddles of water were still present on the flatter portions of the pavement. Occasionally it was difficult to avoid wading through these, and wet footprints marked portions of their route to the square where the bowmen should be waiting for them. How long these would last in the nearly saturated air was a question that bothered Kruger slightly, though Dar did not appear to give it a thought.

They reached the designated point ahead of the others, in spite of the extra time spent in the air. When the force finally arrived no further time was wasted in placing the ambush. That completed, there seemed nothing for Dar and Kruger to do but start exploring buildings.

"I don't see what we're likely to find that will be of much interest," the boy remarked. "We've already been through most of the places around here. We should at least have picked a neighborhood we hadn't explored so thoroughly."

"Then I could not have been sure that it would lend itself to our ambush," pointed out Dar. "I could go only by memory, you know."

"I suppose that's so. Well let's go in here and see what's to be seen." Kruger led the way into a nearby structure and the routine they had developed earlier was repeated. As both had feared there was nothing new about the place above ground, and they both had a healthy dislike of the thought of going below.

And the hours passed. Every so often Dar Lang Ahn went back to the building in which the leader of the bowmen was concealed in order to discuss progress, but there was simply no progress to discuss. Kruger finally stated bluntly that the villagers or their Teachers must have outguessed them, and that the thing to do was take the whole group and proceed directly to the village. The thought, however, seemed to bother his companions seriously; it was not in accord with their instructions.

"We must wait for a time at least," Ten Lee Bar, the leader of the group, insisted.

"But how much time do you have?" retorted Kruger. "It doesn't matter so much to me, I suppose, though I'd like to be on the other side of the ocean before the last of your gliders is grounded for lack of pilots, but if you don't get those books soon you never will and the electrical apparatus that your Teachers want will be a long, long time getting to them."

The native looked uncomfortable.

"In a way, no doubt you are right. Still, if we fail because we did not follow the plan . . ." His voice trailed off for a moment, then he brightened. "I recall that you spoke of electrical equipment here in the city. Could you not use some of the time in obtaining samples of that? I will gladly help." Kruger knew determination when he saw it, even in a nonhuman being. He shrugged.

"It's your funeral. Come along and I'll see what can be found." He turned to the nearest building, Dar Lang Ahn and Ten Lee Bar following him, and led the way through the open entrance hall to one of the inner rooms. Like virtually every other room in the city it had the electric plugs, and with the natives watching, Kruger pried off the covering plates and exposed the connecting wires.

Dar Lang Ahn had heard his explanation before and did not pay as much attention through most of it, but toward the end even he was attracted. This was at the point where Kruger was explaining the need for two conductors and the results that would ensue if any easy path for the current was opened between them. This should have been strictly explanation, since no demonstration material was presumably around; unfortunately, when Ten Lee Bar brought wires together to see what the boy meant the strands of silver suddenly grew red hot, causing him to pull back his hand with a howl of surprised pain.

He was no more surprised than Nils Kruger. For several seconds the boy stared at the glowing wires; then he pried them apart with the insulating handle of his knife.

"Did you just feel heat, or something else?" Kruger asked sharply.

"I don't know. If that was heat I can see why the books have warned us against it." The bowman had his hand at his mouth in an amazingly human fashion.

Realizing he could get no information from a being who did not even know what a burn felt like, Kruger experimented. After drawing a few sparks with his knife blade he concluded that the voltage must be very low. Making sure he was on the dry stone floor—as dry as stone was ever likely to be in this atmosphere, that is— he then bridged the gap with two fingers. He was unable to feel any shock, though a final check with the knife blade showed that the circuit had not picked that moment to go dead.

The question now stared him in the face: did the city normally run on very low voltage *and still have its generators going* or was this the last trickle from some emergency storage system? And also, did the Teachers in the nearby village know about this and was that why they had a general prohibition on the city? Kruger had come to feel a unity with Dar Lang Ahn's people, in spite of the hostility he felt toward their Teachers. If they would not move on their own initiative to obtain the information they needed Nils Kruger would make them! He turned abruptly to Ten Lee Bar.

"This changes matters. Dar Lang Ahn and I are going to that village; things need to be learned. You may come or not with your men, as you see fit."

"But if you go what is the use of our waiting here?"

"I haven't the slightest idea. Use your own judgment. We're on our way." Kruger started out of the building without even asking Dar if he was coming. Ten looked after them for a moment; then he, too, went outside and began to call his group from their hiding places. Looking back just once Kruger saw them starting after him; he smiled to himself but went on without comment.

The trail was easy to follow; they had been over it enough times before. Nothing occurred during the walk. No sign of animal or villager, either by sight or sound, could be detected. Even the clearing of the geysers was silent as they approached it. At the place where the trail forked, sending one branch to the point where they had always talked to the Teachers, Kruger turned toward the pool which had so nearly engulfed them in boiling water. A few moments later the whole party stood before the rock shelter which projected from one side of the rim.

Still the silence was broken only by the scrape of claws on the rock. After waiting for several minutes Kruger went boldly up to the shelter and began to examine it minutely for traces of an entrance. He started on the side toward the water, leaning over the rim to do so, since he had long since convinced himself that the door must be concealed there. However, he found no trace of any crack in the rock. Extending the search to the sides and front produced no better results.

The top was more fruitful. There were, here, a set of fine, almost invisible cracks outlining what might have been a square trapdoor, but the opening thus framed would barely have admitted Dar Lang Ahn himself. Never in the Universe could it have allowed the great body of one of the Teachers to pass. No doubt the books and fire-lighter had gone this way, but where the Teachers went was still a mystery.

Kruger extended the search for many yards around the pool, the rest of the group helping once they understood what he wanted and had overcome their nervousness at the sight of the steaming water. Numerous cracks were found, but all seemed to be random breaks produced by nature. An attempt to see through the small holes through which the Teachers had presumably looked out proved equally futile; none of them was more than a few inches deep. Kruger began to wonder whether the whole thing had not been a huge farce, a deliberate misdirection of attention. Perhaps the Teachers had been watching all the time from the edge of the forest, or some similar vantage point, while the conversations had been going on. In that case where were they now? Still no sign of villagers, still no sound of Teacher's voice—Kruger suddenly felt uneasy.

The others had given up their search and come back to him for further orders as he stood thinking, but he did not stop to feel pleased at having usurped command of the expedition. "Let's go on to the village," he said abruptly, and led the way.

There was no sign of life. They approached the edge of the clearing cautiously, stopping as they saw the first huts. At Kruger's order they spread out, to make poorer targets for possible hidden crossbows, and continued their advance until all were within the village.

Still there was neither sound nor motion. House after house was entered cautiously and searched, all with the same negative result. The place was indeed deserted.

"And I suppose my books went with them!" Dar Lang Ahn topped the conclusion bitterly.

"Seems likely, I'm afraid, unless you want to go back to the pool and pry open that trap door. Of course we still haven't been to the little hut where they reported to their Teachers. Though how a Teacher fitted into that I don't understand, now that I've seen one of them."

"That's not the important point." Dar was off toward the indicated hut like a bolt from his own crossbow. He vanished inside and an instant later called Kruger's name.

"What is it?" asked the boy as he broke into a run toward the hut. "Did they leave your books as a gesture of good will?"

"Not the books. I can't describe the thing." Kruger was inside the door with Dar's last words. For a moment he stopped while his eyes adjusted to the darkness; then he saw what the little pilot meant.

The hut was unfurnished except for a rude table in the center. On that table was lying a piece of apparatus. It was uncased, and contained coils and condensers and what must have been vacuum tubes, all exposed to view. Kruger realized what it must be almost instantly, but he was given no chance to voice his opinion. The device on the table spoke first.

"Come in, Nils Kruger. I have been waiting for you for quite a while. There is much we have to say to each other."

X. ELUCIDATION

THE VOICE was that of the Teacher; there was no mistaking it. Equally, there was no mistaking the fact that Nils Kruger was going to have to revise a number of his ideas. Not even the race which had its headquarters at the ice cap and spread cities over most of the planet had radios, so far as he knew. Could this being have learned more electricity than seemed possible from the deserted city?

"Why were you waiting for me?" asked the boy. "I didn't expect very much to come back, myself—or did you think I needed the fire-lighter too badly to leave it for long?"

"I was sure that Dar Lang Ahn would be back for his books; I know his people too well to doubt that. Later, I knew you would be with him."

"How did you know?"

"I was told. I will explain that in due course. You may not believe it, but in spite of all that I have done which you may resent, I am not entirely your enemy. I am willing to allow you to live as long as your nature permits—provided that certain conditions are met."

"And if they are not?" Kruger naturally resented the hidden being's words.

"Then accidents will continue to happen. You cannot escape all of them."

Slowly the meaning of this dawned on the boy.

"You mean the landslide over by the city, and the pit, were done on purpose?"

"I mean just that. I also mean that a certain door did not lock itself accidentally, and a trap was left unguarded and unlocked with a purpose, and a certain geyser was allowed to feed its outlet instead of a heat exchanger. Be sensible, Kruger; you know too little of this planet, and I know too much."

"But you couldn't—" Kruger stopped; the very fact that this thing knew about the events at the Ice Ramparts made his objection ridiculous. He changed his wording.

"How did you find out? Are you one of the Teachers from there?"

"I talk to them frequently."

"Then did they cause those accidents at your request, or did they want to get rid of me on their own, or did you do it in spite of them?"

"They caused them at my order. They did not want you destroyed; from a purely personal viewpoint neither do I. Unfortunately you are too cooperative."

"In what way? And why should that be a point against me?"

"I asked you many questions while you were a prisoner here, not only about yourself but about the technical knowledge you have. You answered them all, truthfully and, as far as I was able to tell, correctly. I am not an electrician myself, but I know enough to follow most of what you said."

"What is your objection to that?"

"If you tell me, whom you had no reason to trust, you will presumably tell Dar Lang Ahn's people. I have no objection to the state of civilization which they now enjoy, but there are good and sufficient reasons why we do not want them to match the technology of your people."

"How do you know what our technical level is?"

"You told me enough yourself merely by being here."

"What is your objection to their learning our technology, if you learn it too?"

"Principally, we do not want them to leave this planet. We need them here." Kruger began to develop a strong suspicion at this point and asked a question designed to check it.

"How about these people of yours who were here in the village? Would you object to their learning?"

"Very much. They are easier to control as they are."

"How is it that you dare tell me all this with Dar Lang Ahn listening to the conversation?"

"His Teachers know it already. They did not want to help me get rid of you, but I was able to bring pressure to bear. When their attempts failed I had them send you back here, to be persuaded if possible, destroyed if not."

Kruger, convinced that his idea was right, leaned forward and spoke with more anger than he had felt in his previous life. "That does it. You are not the same race as Dar's people or as the people who lived in this village. You have the villagers to do as you want in the way of everyday labor, and the rest pretty much the same thing in more complicated matters. I don't know whether you or they are the original inhabitants of this world, but I can certainly see why you don't want them to leave it now. You might have to do some of your own work! Isn't that it?" Kruger was so furious by the time he reached the end of this speech that it was a wonder the hidden being could understand him, but it apparently did.

"You are partly right," it answered calmly.

"Partly! I'm right from soup to nuts. I dare you to let me see you! "

"I'm afraid that's not possible just now."

"Why not? Afraid I'll step on you?"

"Not quite that. However, our meeting under the same conditions would indeed result in the death of one of us. I could not survive in your environment and I am pretty sure you could not in mine—at least Dar Lang Ahn certainly could not."

"Then he, and not you, is one of the natives of this world. You came and conquered it!"

"I do not know enough of the past to refute that belief, but I have reason to doubt it."

"It's certainly plain enough."

"You make an extremely positive statement on remarkably little data. Would you be willing to promise not to reveal any knowledge to Dar Lang Ahn's people, except what we approve—"

"No!"

"Let me finish—until you have learned enough about us to form a balanced opinion?"

"Who decides when my opinion is balanced?"

"I would agree to release you from your promise whenever you asked, with the understanding that I might then find it expedient or necessary to dispose of you."

"How do you know I'll feel bound by a promise obtained under such terms?"

"I should not advise you to do or say anything which would give me reason to doubt the value of your word. I am sure you can see why."

"How about Dar?"

"As I said, he may say what he wishes while he lives. He has no knowledge that I object to his people's sharing."

"He heard me discuss electricity with you."

"I remember."

"All right, I will say nothing without giving you fair warning, but I assure you that you have some heavy convincing to do." Something very like a sigh of relief came through the speaker.

"I much prefer it that way," was the answer. "Believe it or not, I would like to be on the same terms with you that Dar Lang Ahn seems to be."

"After those engineered accidents that will take some doing—and some believing."

"Your words make me begin to wonder whether your race can possibly be one that never makes mistakes. Mine is not. However, I had better get to my job of explanation.

"In the first place, your idea that we simply use Dar Lang Ahn's race for labor is quite wrong. It would be practically impossible for us to do that, since we cannot live under the same conditions they do. Their death, in a few years now, will mark the time when we can live normally on this world."

"You mean you live during the time they die, and—"

"And most of us die during the time they live. That is correct."

"Then that city between the volcanoes was built by your people!"

"It was. It is maintained, during our death time, by a few people of whom I am one."

"So that's why the electricity was on in that building."

"When? Just now?"

"Yes, when we were in the city just before coming here." A succession of sounds quite beyond the power of human vocal cords to imitate spluttered from the speaker, and was followed by a brief silence. Then the invisible creature spoke again.

"Thank you. I had to turn on the power some time ago to handle a steam valve—I have you to thank for that, I suspect—and forgot to turn it off again. My own life is well past its prime, I fear."

"You mean that thing in the crater across the city—you were handling that?"

"Not at first; it is automatic. The steam comes from the same underground heat source that maintains the geysers. The heat is virtually inexhaustible, but the water is not. I had to shut the valve manually because the loss of steam was threatening most of our other machinery. Am I correct in suspecting that you are the cause of the inconvenience?"

"I'm afraid so." Kruger told the story, his good humor returning as he did so.

"I understand," the other said at the end. "I trust you will take the time to remove those stones before you go back to the ice cap. I could get my people here to do it, I suppose, but there are reasons why I do not want them there yet."

"I'm willing as long as your manual valve stays off," replied Kruger.

"We seem to be trusting each other," was the answer. "However, let us get back to the subject. As I said, we are different from your friends; we live under different conditions, use different tools, different buildings, different foods. In short, we do not compete with them—we might almost as well be living on a different planet."

"Then what is your objection to *their* living on a different planet—or at least being able to do so?"

"That is as much in their interest as ours, as any of their Teachers will tell you. If they left this planet how likely would they be to find another just like it?"

"I don't know; there must be quite a number of them. There are vast numbers of planets in the galaxy."

"But very few, if any, which would kill them at the proper time. I have gathered that you do not know when you are to die, and like it that way. Did you ever try to find out how your friend Dar would feel under such circumstances?" Kruger was silent; he had gathered already that Dar rather pitied the human state of eternal uncertainty. Then he remembered one of his numerous pet theories.

"I admit that Dar has been educated all his life to the idea that dying at a certain particular time is natural and inevitable, but it seems to be just a matter of education—some of his race seem to face quite happily the prospect of living longer."

"They did not tell you that at the Ice Ramparts." Kruger chose to interpret this answer as an admission that he was right.

"They didn't have to; I'm not blind. All Dar Lang Ahn's people, even your branch of them here, are the same size —and the same age. Their Teachers are also of a size, but much larger than Dar. It didn't take a genius to see the story: either these people grow throughout their lives, or else this dying time you talk about comes before they reach their full growth. Some live through that time, and keep on growing. They are the Teachers."

"You are quite right in the main facts, but I think your

114

remark about the attitude of the Teachers toward their prolonged lives must have been guesswork. Did you actually talk to any of the people at the Ice Ramparts who will be the Teachers for the next time of living?"

"What do you mean? I talked to a lot of their Teachers."

"But surely you do not think that the present group of Teachers will live through this time of dying! The fact that they are all of a size, as you said, should show you that. The next group will come from among the people who started to live at the same time Dar Lang Ahn did."

"But how were they chosen? Why cannot Dar here join them?"

"He could, but I am sure he does not wish to. The Ice Ramparts are the only place on Abyormen where his kind can live during the time my people hold the planet. They simply cannot accommodate the whole race; some selection must be made. Since long training is needed they are selected early in life."

"You suggested that those chosen are not too happy about it. I find that hard to believe."

"A chosen Teacher accepts from a sense of duty. Living beyond the natural time exacts a penalty; you saw that the Teachers at the Ice Ramparts moved slowly when they moved at all. You did not see them all; three out of four, by this time, are virtually cripples. Their size increases, but their strength does not keep up with it. Their joints become stiff, their digestion untrustworthy. Physical ills develop which make life far more of a burden than a pleasure. They accept this lot because if they did not each new group of their people would have to start from the beginning, and this world, during their time of living, would be inhabited by nothing but wild animals."

"Is the same true for the Teachers of your race?"

"It is. However, I am not as near the end of my duty as are those at the ice cap; I must last through, or nearly through, my people's next time of living. Life is not too bad for me, so far."

115

"But just what are the differences between your races? And what change in conditions kills off one and starts the other growing? Does it affect any other life forms on the planet?"

"The first question is difficult to answer unless we can work out some means of your seeing me, and I don't know how that would be possible. My environment would have to be separated from yours to permit us both to live, and I know of no barrier through which we could see." Kruger started to suggest glass or quartz and discovered he did not know the word for either substance. Before he could invent a sentence to describe them the voice went on, "The change in conditions is pretty thorough, but the most important factor is temperature. It gets much hotter (Kruger whistled gently) and the air changes."

"Do you breathe air, or water, or both?" asked the boy. "Your city extends into the ocean."

"Only at the moment. During our living time the oceans disappear almost completely. We suppose that they travel as vapor to that portion of Abyormen on which neither sun shines and are there precipitated in either liquid or solid state. We have not been able to explore such regions, for fairly obvious reasons, but knowledge of the conditions at the Ice Ramparts lends support to this theory."

"But the sun Arren shines on the Ramparts, most of the time."

"Just now, yes; the region I mentioned is a quarter of the way around the planet from the point you speak of."

"I begin to get the situation," Kruger said. "I had already realized that Abyormen was traveling in a pretty eccentric orbit around Theer; if what you say is correct Theer itself is doing much the same around Arren."

"So we have deduced, though the precise size and shape of the path is not known for certain. We have been unable to devise measuring devices which would give us the needed values. We are sure, however, that both suns

116

are much larger than Abyormen and very distant from it, so it seems reasonable to suppose that Abyormen rather than the suns is moving."

"I can see the sort of thing that must happen to this place; I suppose my last question was wasted—if the temperature changes as you say, it must affect all the life on the planet. I've wondered why most of the trees and animals of a particular species seemed to be about the same size, now it's quite reasonable. Most of them must have started growing at about the same time."

"I take it that this is not the case on your world." The words were half a question. Kruger spent some time describing the seasonal changes of Earth and the way in which various forms of life adapted to them.

"It seems, then," was the Teacher's comment to this information, "that most of your creatures either continue through the full year at more or less normal activity, or else become dormant for the unsuitable season. On this world the first is not possible, at least not for us, and I find it hard to imagine a creature able to stand the full extremes of Abyormen's climate. The second seems to me to be extremely wasteful; if one type of life cannot stand the situation for part of the year why should not another take its place during that period?"

"It seems sensible," admitted Kruger.

"Then what objection do you have to my race's sharing Abyormen with Dar Lang Ahn's?"

"None whatever. What bothers me is your treatment of them, forbidding me to tell them enough of the physical sciences to let them get out from under your control. You certainly don't seem to mind my giving *you* all the information I can."

"To me personally, no. To my people, I would have the same objection that I do for Dar Lang Ahn's."

"You mean you don't want your *own* people to be able to build space ships, supposing I were able to tell them how?"

"I mean just that."

"But that doesn't make sense. What objection could you have to some of your people's *wanting* to go off and leave Dar's folk alone?"

"I said long ago that we need Dar's race, though you chose to interpret my words differently. What is more, his people need ours just as badly, even though Dar Lang Ahn doesn't know it—his Teachers do, at least."

"Then why don't you treat them as friends instead of inferiors?"

"They are friends. I feel a particularly strong attachment for Dar Lang Ahn; that is one reason you were so well treated while you were in this place before, and why I sent my villagers away rather than risk violence when you came this time."

"If you are so fond of Dar—whom you have never seen before in your life, as nearly as I can see—why did you keep his books? That has bothered him more than anything else that has happened since I have known him."

"That was for experimental reasons, I am afraid. I wanted to learn more about you. I am sorry that Dar Lang Ahn suffered, but I am glad to have learned something of your capacity for sympathy and friendship. His books will be on the trap at the place where we used to talk as soon as I can get them there after ending this conversation."

"How about my fire-lighter?"

"Do you really want it? I took it apart, I'm afraid, and am not sure that I could get it back together again. The condenser (he had to stop to explain this word) was, of course, quite familiar to us, but the part that turns the sun's heat into electricity was not. If you can spare it my scientists would be interested—when we have some."

"I thought you didn't want your people to learn too much."

"I don't, but I seriously doubt that this particular device will get any of them off the planet. I judge that it is less practical for our purposes than the generators we already use, which tap the volcanic heat of Abyormen."

"Then you are living underground, near volcanoes where it is hot enough to suit you? I should think from what I saw of this continent that a good many of you must live through the cold time."

"I am underground, as you say, but there are not many of us. Only four live in this area; similar numbers are in each of our other cities."

"But you must have a lot more room to live in during your bad season than the others do. They're cramped under that ice cap—"

"Which is many hundreds of miles across at its smallest. It would be possible to dig caverns and, probably, store food enough for most if not all of the race."

"And there are volcanoes for I don't know how many hundreds of miles down the length of that peninsula I followed from the place I was left. In short, there doesn't seem to be any reason why both races can't live at full strength all the time. What's wrong with the idea?"

"I have been giving you hints as to what is wrong with it all through this conversation. I told you each race was necessary to the other; you seem to believe that is due to our laziness. I mentioned that other planets would be unsuitable because they would not kill us at the right time; you appear to have put that down to superstition. I tell you that I have a strong personal interest in Dar Lang Ahn's welfare, and apparently you simply don't believe it. You remark on your own that there is no technical impossibility, or even great difficulty, in our remaining alive throughout the year if we choose. Instead of putting all those items together, you treat them as a group of separate impossibilities. I confess I have been trying ever since this conversation started to get some sort of idea of human intelligence, and you are certainly not giving me a high one. Can you honestly not think of an explanation that will embrace all those facts?"

Kruger frowned, and no one spoke for a minute or so; then Dar Lang Ahn made a remark.

"If you are testing intelligence, Teacher, you'd better

compare his with mine. I've lived on Abyormen all my life and don't see what you're driving at."

"Your training would prevent it."

"Then I'd like to think that mine does the same thing," snapped Kruger, somewhat annoyed. "Why should I be able to win your guessing game if he can't?"

"Very well, I do not wish to cause you anger. The explanation will, I think, be easiest if you give me some words in your language. I understand that individuals of your race are directly concerned with the production of other individuals. What is the newly produced being called?"

"A child—son or daughter, according to—"

"The general term will be enough. Is there a word describing the relationship of two childs produced by the same individual?"

"Brother or sister, according—"

"All right, I will assume either word is usable. I have no child, since I am still alive, but Dar Lang Ahn is a child of my brother."

The silence was much longer this time, while Nils Kruger fitted piece after piece of the jigsaw puzzle into place, and his attitude grew from one of sheer disbelief, through gradual recognition of the possibilities, to acceptance. "You win—Uncle!" he said weakly, at last. "But I still don't see—"

Kruger's sentence was interrupted—and not by the Teacher.

"I think I'll say 'uncle' too." The voice was a slow drawl that the boy had never to his knowledge heard before, but it was speaking English. "I can stand," it went on, "an occasional word that sounds like good old English in any collection of random noises, and will gladly put it down to coincidence. However, when 'child,' 'son,' 'daughter,' 'brother,' 'sister,' and 'uncle' all occur within the same thirty-second period, coincidence goes a long, long way out the window. Mr. Nils Kruger, if you've been contributing heavily to the conversations we've been recording for the last couple of weeks, I hope you've developed a good accent. If not, a couple of philologists I know are going to be very, very angry indeed!"

XI. ASTRONOMY; DIPLOMACY

MOST HUMAN beings continue hoping long after any logical excuse for it has died. The man going into battle against impossible odds, the pilot who stays with a blazing airplane to guide it away from a city, the condemned criminal in the death cell—few of them give up while they breathe. Nils Kruger had not entirely relinquished hope of seeing Earth again. He did not, however, expect to be rescued. He had had faint ideas, which he would have admitted himself were illogical, that perhaps by combining Abyormenite technology with his own some sort of ship able to cross the five hundred light years to the solar system might be built. Even after he had gained a fairly accurate idea of the technical limitations of Dar Lang Ahn's race the thought had not entirely vanished; but unreasonable as he may have been in this respect, he never for an instant supposed that another terrestrial space ship would approach the Pleiades during his lifetime. There was too much else for them to do.

As a result the sound of an unmistakably human voice cutting in on his conversation with a creature who could hardly be less human gave Kruger quite literally the shock of his life. For some moments he was completely unable to speak. Several questions came from the radio, and when these were answered only by Dar Lang Ahn's rather unfortunate attempts at English the disturbance in the distant space ship was nearly as great as that in the hut.

"That can't be Kruger—he wouldn't talk like that, and anyway he's dead!"

"But where could they have learned English?"

"My year-old kid speaks better English than that!"

"Kruger, is that you or has the philology department gone off the rails?"

"I—I'm here all right, but you shouldn't do things like that. What ship is that? and how come you were listening in? and what are you doing in the Pleiades anyway?"

"It's your own ship, the *Alphard;* this is Donabed. That radio you have is pretty sad; I'm not sure of your voice either. We've been here a couple of weeks, and have been picking up and recording all the radio noise we could find in hopes of having some of the language in useful shape when we landed. I'm glad you were too sensible to expect us back; it seems that there's something about this system that had thrown the astronomers into fits, and they had to come back to look for themselves. Is that radio a native product, or did you make it?"

"Strictly home grown." Kruger was back in control of himself, though his knees still felt weak. "Just a minute, we have an audience that doesn't speak English." Kruger shifted back into the Abyormenite speech and explained to Dar and the Teacher what had happened. "Now, while you're coming down, will you please explain to me just what is so peculiar about this place from the astronomer's point of view?"

"I'm not an astrophysicist, but here's the situation as I understand it," returned Donabed. "You know the elementary facts about the sources of stellar energy, and that main-sequence stars like the sun and this red dwarf should be able to keep radiating at their present rate for billions of years. However, there are a lot of stars in space which are a lot more luminous than Sol, sometimes by a factor of tens of thousands. Suns like that are using up their hydrogen so rapidly that they should not be able to last more than a few million, or a few tens of millions, of years at the most. Alcyone, like several other stars in the Pleiades, is such a sun.

"So far, that's all right. The Pleiades cluster is full of nebulous material, and presumably that is still combining to form other stars to add to the hundreds already in the

122

group; but here we run into trouble. They've worked out to a fair degree of precision the sort of things that should happen to the condensing clouds. In some circumstances, with a certain amount of angular momentum, you can expect several stars to form, traveling in orbits about each other—a regular binary or multiple star system. In other cases, with less angular momentum, you get most of the mass in one star and the dregs left over forming a planetary system. It's a little surprising, though not impossible, to get a double or multiple star with planets as well; but to get a star like Alcyone with planets anywhere near it is queer as all get-out! A sun like that is putting out radiation tens of thousands of times as intense as Sol's; that radiation exerts pressure; and that pressure should easily be sufficient to push out of the neighborhood any solid particles that had any idea of coalescing into planets. That's one of the things that can be computed and checked experimentally, and it's hard to get around. For that reason the star-gazers were not too bothered when they found from our data that Alcyone had a red dwarf companion, but when they learned that the companion had a planet they went wild. We had quite a time persuading some of them that we hadn't made some sort of silly mistake; we had to point out that we'd actually landed on the thing."

"I'll say we did!" Kruger muttered.

"You should know. By the way, its name is officially Kruger, if you care."

"I'm afraid its name is Abyormen, if we follow accepted usage," replied the boy. "But go on."

"There's not much more to tell. They hated like poison to give up their pet theories, and I've heard them speculating all the way out here about the possibility of the red sun's having been captured by Alcyone after its planet or planets formed, and so on. There's lots of work to be done, and you can help a lot. I judge you've learned a good deal of the local language, and will save our time by acting as an interpreter."

"Yes, up to a point; somehow whenever I talk to one of these people we get crossed up sooner or later. It may be happening without my even knowing it right now, since I haven't even seen this fellow I've been talking to on the radio."

"How's that? Haven't seen him?"

"No, and haven't the faintest idea what he looks like. Look, Major, if you'll come down and get me out of this steam bath I'll be a lot better able to explain all this and, believe me, it will take quite a bit of explaining."

"We're on the way. Will you be coming up alone?" Kruger explained the question briefly to Dar and asked if he would care to go along. The native was a trifle dubious for a moment, then realized that more book material would undoubtedly be involved and agreed to accompany his friend.

"Dar Lang Ahn will come with me," Kruger reported to Donabed.

"Will he need any special accommodation?"

"I've seen him perfectly comfortable on an ice field, and he's made glider flights of fully two days without bothering to drink, so I don't think temperature and humidity will bother him. I don't know about pressure; as you say, it's higher here."

"How high does he go on these glider flights?"

"I don't know. He hasn't any flight instruments, by our standards."

"Did he ever get up near the top of the usual cumulus clouds?"

"Yes. I've been with him. He gets as high as he can whenever he can on long-distance flights."

"All right. I don't think terrestrial pressure will hurt him. You'd better explain the risks to him if you can, though, and let him make his own decision."

Kruger was never actually sure whether Dar completely understood him or not, but he was standing beside Kruger when the *Alphard's* landing tender settled into the clearing of the geysers. The Teacher had been informed of what was going on, and the boy had promised to resume contact with him on the ship's radio equipment as soon as was practical. The hidden being had made no objection, though he must have realized that the move was taking Kruger out of his reach.

The flight back to the *Alphard*, which was circling safely beyond Abyormen's atmosphere, was uneventful to all except Dar Lang Ahn. He did not ask a single question while it lasted, but his eyes took in everything there was to see. One peculiarity of his behavior was noticed by most of the human crew. In most cases when a more or less primitive creature is taken for a ride off his planet he spends most of the time looking at the world as seen from outside. Nearly all Dar's attention, on the other hand, was devoted to the structure and handling of the tender. The only time he looked down for more than a moment at a time was when circular velocity was reached and the tender went weightless. Then he looked back at the surface for nearly a minute and, to the sincere astonishment of all watchers, took the phenomenon in his stride. Apparently he had convinced himself that the falling sensation did not represent an actual fall or, if it did, that the pilots would take care of the situation before it became dangerous. Major Donabed developed a healthy respect for Dar Lang Ahn in that moment; he had experienced too many educated human beings who had become hysterical in like circumstances.

Of course, reflected the boy, Dar is a flyer and gets plenty of brief low-weight jolts when he hits downdrafts or reaches the tops of updrafts, but they never last more than a second or two. The fellow was good; Kruger himself, after nearly an earthly year on the ground, was feeling a trifle queasy.

In due course the monstrous bulk of the *Alphard* was sighted, approached, and contacted, and the tender eased into the hull through its special lock. The group disembarked and a conference was called at once.

The meeting was held in the ship's largest lounge, since

everyone wanted to hear Kruger's story. By common consent he made his report first, passing briefly over the way he had escaped death at the time he was abandoned and dwelling on his experiences as they applied to the plants, animals, minerals, and people of Abyormen. The lack of anything resembling fruit, the fact that the stems of many plants were edible but not very nourishing, the chances he had taken to find that they were at least not poisonous, and his determination to leave the hot, volcano-ridden area where he had been left and make his way to the pole, where it might be more comfortable, were woven into a reasonably concise account. Everyone who listened had some question or other when he was finished, however, and it was necessary for the *Alphard's* commander to act as chairman.

"You must have had a bit of trouble setting up your direction, when you first started to travel." This was one of the astronomers.

"It was a bit confusing." Kruger smiled. "If the red sun had merely kept changing in size it wouldn't have been bad, but it wobbled back and forth, at the place where I landed, from southeast to southwest and back again, in a way that took me quite a while to get used to. The blue one was easier—Alcyone rises in the east and sets in the west the way things ought to. At least, it does that far from the pole, and it was easy enough to see why it didn't when I got further north."

"Right. The red dwarf's motions are natural enough, if you remember how eccentric the planet's orbit is. How much does the libration amount to, in your experience? I've only seen the planet through about one revolution."

"I'd say about sixty degrees each side of the mean."

The astronomer nodded, and yielded the floor. The captain gave the nod to a geologist.

"You say nearly all the country you saw was volcanic?"

"On the continent where you found me, yes. Actually I didn't cover too much of the planet, remember. The long peninsula I followed north—"

"About three thousand miles," interjected a photographer.

"Thanks. Its full length was actively volcanic, and the continental region it projected from is largely covered with lava flows of various ages. Near the ice cap it's mountainous but not obviously volcanic."

"Good. We've got to map some stratigraphic sequences as soon as possible, if we're to get any idea of the age of this world. I don't suppose you saw any fossils near the ice?"

"I was only on the ground near the settlement; I flew over the rest. Dar Lang Ahn, here, could probably help you, though."

"Would he be willing to?"

"Probably. His curiosity bump is quite prominent. I gave you an idea of what he wants knowledge for— he puts it in books for the next generation, since his own won't last much longer." Kruger did not smile as he said this; the prospect of losing Dar was weighing on him more and more heavily as time drew on.

"Would your friend tell us a little more about this alternation-of-generations business?" asked the biologist. "We have animals on Earth that do much the same, though usually the two forms are not adapted to such drastically different environments, but the thing that bothers me right now is the question of these Teachers. When they finally do die, is the result a crop of the alternate-type descendant, or nothing, or what?"

"I don't know, and neither does Dar Lang Ahn. You'd better ask that 'hot' form Teacher I was talking to when you heard me. I don't even know whether there is one offspring or a number of them in the normal state of affairs."

"That's obvious enough—if there were only one, with no other method of reproduction the race would have died off long ago. There must be occasional accidental deaths."

"Well, the person to ask is the Teacher, anyway. I'll do it for you when I talk to him."

"Why do the Teachers keep most of their people in ignorance of this business, anyway?" Another questioner took over.

"You'll have to ask them. If I were in their place I'd do it to keep the peace, but this one claims that they don't mind having a definite death date."

"I'd like to talk to your friend about it."

"All right. I suspect someone will have to set up a schedule sheet, though." The questions and answers went on and on, until Kruger gave up trying to stifle his yawns. The commander finally broke up the meeting; but even then the boy did not rest for some time. He proceeded to show Dar Lang Ahn over the *Alphard,* answering his little friend's questions as best he could.

He finally slept, enjoying weightlessness for the first time in many months. He did not notice whether or not Dar was able to sleep in the circumstances, but the native appeared adequately refreshed in the morning, so Kruger assumed that he had. Dar refused to try human foods, insisting he was not hungry, but Kruger consumed a breakfast so huge as to move some of his acquaintances to warn him. The relatively low nourishment value of Abyormenite plants had gradually accustomed him to eating far larger quantities at a meal while he was on the planet.

Hunger satisfied, he reported to the commander, who immediately called another conference, this time of scientists only. It was decided that top priority on Dar's time should be given the philologists, so that more interpreters would be available as soon as possible. The biologists were advised to take a landing boat and catch some animals of their own; they would have to get most of their knowledge the hard way. Kruger soothed them by promising to help them with the Teacher while Dar was giving language lessons.

The geologists, however, were going to need Dar's personal assistance. They could, of course, map the whole land surface of Abyormen and start checking likely spots for sedimentary outcrops in person, but the time which would be consumed that way could be put to much better uses. In consequence, Dar was shown colored pictures of the sorts of rock the specialists hoped to find and asked if he knew any places on the planet where they might be found.

Unfortunately he failed to recognize a single picture. The geologists might have given up after exhausting their photographs and gone back to the map plan, but Kruger noticed that one of the pictures was of a sample of travertine virtually identical with the material deposited around the geyser pool. He pointed this out to Dar.

"Your pictures are not very good," was the response.

Twenty minutes later it had been established that Dar Lang Ahn could see light ranging in wave length from forty-eight hundred Angstroms to just under eighteen thousand—that is, not quite as far to violet as the average human being but more than an octave farther into the infra-red. The color pictures, balancing the three primary shades to make combinations which reproduced what the human eye saw of the original, simply did not duplicate more than half the color range that Dar saw. As he said, the color pictures were no good. The dyes in the film were the wrong colors, in that part of the spectrum.

"No wonder I never did get any of his words for colors," muttered Kruger disgustedly. The problem was solved by making black and white prints and letting Dar concentrate on texture. Thereafter he was able to identify more than half the pictures and to tell where samples of most of them could be found. After a short geology lesson he even suggested areas of thrust and block-faulting and canyons which exposed strata to depths of hundreds or thousands of feet; the maps he drew were more than sufficient to enable the regions in question to be located. The rock specialists were delighted. So was Dar Lang Ahn, and so was Nils Kruger—the last for reasons of his own.

The boy had resumed radio contact with the Teacher while this was going on and told him everything that had happened. He explained what the visitors wanted in the way of information and offered to trade as much knowledge as the creature wanted. Unfortunately the Teacher still felt that too much scientific knowledge was not good for his people. He would not budge from his point that knowledge would, in time, lead to space travel, and space travel would inevitably lead to disruption of the Abyormenite life cycle, since it was ridiculous to suppose that another planet could match Abyormen's characteristics.

"But your people don't have to *stay* on other planets; why not just visit, to trade or learn or simply look?"

"I have showed you, Nils Kruger, that your ignorance of my people led you far astray before. Please believe me when I tell you that you are equally in error to think that leaving this world could help them in any way." He remained stubborn on that point, and Kruger had to give up.

He reported his failure to Commander Burke and was somewhat surprised at that officer's answer.

"Aren't you just as fortunate that he didn't accept your offer?"

"Why, sir?"

"As I understand it you were virtually promising him any of our technical knowledge in which he might feel an interest. I admit that we are not as security conscious as we were a few generations ago when Earth still had wars, but it's generally considered inadvisable to be too free with a new race in the matter of potentially destructive techniques until we know them pretty well."

"But I do know them!"

"I'll admit that you know Dar Lang Ahn. You have met a few others of his race, a number of his Teachers, and have spoken by radio to a Teacher of what I suppose we'll have to call the complementary race. I refuse to credit you with 'knowing' the people in general, and still claim that you might have been in a rather equivocal position had that creature accepted your offer."

130

"But you didn't object to everyone's telling Dar all he asked about."

"For about the same reason that Teacher didn't object to your telling him."

"You mean because he's going to die soon? Won't you let him go back to the Ice Ramparts before then? He expects to."

"I suppose he does. I don't think it will do any harm; he will take no written material, and without that I am sure he could do no damage."

Kruger checked himself; he had been on the verge of mentioning the native's memory. He wanted Dar Lang Ahn to learn things. He knew that what the little native was told or shown he would remember, and what he remembered he would tell his Teachers at the Ice Ramparts. The Teacher at the village might object, but there seemed little he could do; Kruger had kept their bargain.

But could that being do something? He had claimed to have influence over the Teachers at the ice cap—enough to make them attempt to murder Kruger against their own wills. Perhaps he could force them to ignore the information Dar brought, or even destroy Dar; that was definitely not part of Kruger's plan. What was the influence the being possessed, anyway? Could anything be done to reduce or eliminate it? He would have to talk to that Teacher again—and plan the talk very, very carefully indeed. The boy floated motionless for a long time, thinking, but at last his expression brightened a trifle. A few moments later he shoved himself into motion against the nearest wall and headed for the communication room.

The Teacher acknowledged the call at once.

"I suppose you have thought of some more arguments why I should favor the spread of your technology?"

"Not exactly," replied Kruger. "I wanted to ask a question or two. You said that there were four of you Teachers at that city. I'd like to know whether the others share your attitude in this matter."

"They do." The answer was prompt and disconcerted the boy a trifle.

"All right. How about the Teachers in the other cities? I assume you have been telling them about all that has been happening." This time the answer was not so prompt.

"As a matter of fact, we have not. We do not maintain constant communication; simply check with each other every year. If I were to call now they would probably not be listening. It does not matter; there is no doubt how they would feel. After all, we have maintained for many long years the policy of limiting technology for ourselves and making sure that we were the source of knowledge for the others—the radios they have at the Ice Ramparts were made by us, for example; they do not know how to do it."

"I see." The cadet was a trifle discouraged but by no means ready to give up. "Then you would not mind our visiting the other cities and contacting your fellow Teachers directly, to put the proposition to them." He fervently hoped that it would not occur to the other to ask whether the human beings were all in accord on the matter.

"Certainly. You would, of course, explain the situation as you have to me; they would give the same answer."

Kruger smiled wickedly.

"Yes, we might do that, or we might tell them a slightly different story—say, that your mind has become affected some way, and you had tricked some information out of us and were tired of the sacrifices involved in being a Teacher, and were going to build devices that would keep a larger part of the planet hot and stop your people's time of dying—"

"I never heard such nonsense in my whole year of life!"

"Of course you haven't. Neither have your friends in other cities. *But how will they know it's nonsense?* Will they dare take the chance?" He paused, but no answer came from the radio. "I still think that there's no need for your people to fly off into space just because they learn

132

a little physics. Aren't they as capable of seeing the dangers involved as you are?"

"Wait. I must think." Silence reigned for many minutes, broken only by a faint crackle of static. Kruger waited tensely.

"You have taught me something, human being." The Teacher's voice finally sounded again. "I will not tell you what it is. But Dar Lang Ahn's Teachers may learn what they can." He said no more.

Kruger relaxed, with a grin spreading over his face. The plan would work; it couldn't fail, now.

Dar Lang Ahn would soak up vast quantities of information, enough to fill many books—books which could not possibly be written before the time of dying. Dar Lang Ahn would return to the Ice Ramparts with his knowledge, and he would still be dictating it or writing it himself when the time came to seal the caverns against the rising temperature and changing atmosphere. He would still be inside when that happened, not out in the cities of the "cold" people dying with his fellows. Dar Lang Ahn, by sheer necessity, would become a Teacher; and Nils Kruger would not lose his little friend.

XII. GEOLOGY; ARCHAEOLOGY

ABYORMEN IS larger than the earth and has a smaller percentage of sea area even in the cold time, so the geologists had a great deal of territory to cover. They did not, of course, attempt to do it all; the basic plan was to attempt enough stratigraphic correlation to get a fair idea of its geological history and, if at all possible, find datable radioactives in the series far enough down to get at least a minimum value for the age of the planet. The last was all the astronomers really wanted, but the biologists had considerably higher standards. They came along, prepared to analyze any fossils found by every technique known to their field.

Layer after layer of sedimentary rock was traced, sometimes for miles underground, sometimes only yards before it vanished—perhaps because quakes had shuffled it into a puzzle that took experience to solve, perhaps because the phenomena which had deposited it in the first place had covered only a limited area and the formation pinched out naturally. A limestone bed laid down over a million square miles at the bottom of a sea is one thing; a sandstone lens that was once the delta of a stream running into a small lake is something else—sometimes a rather inconvenient something else, when a problem of relative dates is in question.

Kruger thanked his luck that Commander Burke was not with this ground party and prayed constantly that he would not overhear any remarks made by the geologists, for Dar Lang Ahn was learning a good deal of English as time went on, and there are few places where a photographic memory can make itself more obvious or useful than in a stratigraphy problem. The geologists without

134

exception regarded the native with awe and felt a friendship for him comparing strongly with Kruger's own. Sooner or later the commander would learn; the boy hoped that by then his little friend's popularity would have reached a point where the old officer would be moved to get rid of his suspicions.

Nowhere on the planet did there seem to be structures corresponding with the "shields" which characterize certain parts of Earth. Apparently all the present land surface had been submerged in the not too distant past; there was more than a suggestion that Abyormen suffered much more seismic and orogenic activity than Earth. One of the specialists suggested that a reason for this might lie in the "Long Year" seasonal changes, when the greater part of the sea water was deposited on the ice caps. A seismic check of the cap in the southern hemisphere (*not* over the south pole) indicated a thickness of nearly thirty-five thousand feet. It was snowing at the time the check was made, Theer never shone on this part of the planet, and Arren would not rise for several terrestrial years.

While several of Abyormen's short years passed before any absolute dating of strata was possible, the astronomers learned what they had feared rather quickly. From the beginning, of course, the geologists had kept their eyes open for pegmatites and other igneous intrusions which might contain radioactives suitable for dating, and fairly soon these were found at several places on the continent they were examining. It was not possible to correlate these rocks with the sedimentaries, at the time, but one of them had a uranium-lead ratio corresponding to an age of just under one and a half billion years. It was a large sample, and ten independent checks were run, none varying more than about twenty million years from the mean. Since the astronomers were not willing to believe that Alcyone had been in existence longer than something like one per cent of that time they accepted the information a trifle glumly.

But dated or not, the sedimentaries had their own fields of interest. If Dar Lang Ahn had ever seen a fossil in his

135

life he had never given it a second thought. This omission was easily remedied, for the sediments had their share of organic remains. A lens of limestone some two hundred miles across, near the center of the continent, seemed to consist largely of a reef deposit, and several hundred different species were found at various points within it. Shellfish that might have come straight from Earth were present by the thousands—at least, so it appeared to Kruger; a biologist spent much time pointing out technical differences.

"I suppose," he finished, "that you could find a good many creatures virtually identical with these on the shores of your present oceans. There seems to be some ability in the mollusks and their relatives to ride out the changes of a planet. On Earth they've been around for half a billion years—changed, to be sure, but the basic plan seems to keep right on going."

"I understand you in all but one point," Dar Lang Ahn replied in his slow, careful English. "I have been with you all along here, and have seen fossils like this in many different layers of rock, as you say is reasonable, but I have never seen a living creature which in any way resembles those fossils."

"Have you ever spent any length of time at the seashore?"

"Much. Nils Kruger and I walked along one for about three hundred miles recently, if the occasions in my previous eight hundred years don't count."

"That's right!" Kruger exclaimed excitedly. "I knew there was something funny about that beach and never could put my finger on it. There weren't any seashells, or stranded jellyfish, or anything of that nature. No wonder it looked queer!"

"Hmph. I confess that is distinctly odd. How about other sea creatures?"

"I don't know. I think there are animals of various sorts living in the water, and I'm sure there are plants. I can't think of very many different kinds, though." The biologist gave this bit of information to those of his colleagues engaged in field work; he himself was too busy with fossil correlation to follow it up.

Gradually he established order out of the chaos. For purposes of discussion, he divided Abyormen's past into periods whose boundaries in time seemed to have been established by the general flooding of this continent which had resulted in the limestone beds. The geologists could not find evidence for definite periods of mountain-building, which are usually better for such a purpose; on Abyormen, as they had already suspected, orogenic activity seemed to be fairly uniformly distributed through time.

There were, of course, many reasons why the world might be more active seismically than Earth. It was larger, for one thing—ninety-one hundred miles in diameter and forty per cent more massive, so that a one hundred seventy pound man weighed about one hundred eighty on its surface. The percentage difference was small, but the total tonnage of gravitational forces available for orogeny was much larger than on mankind's home world. At any rate there was the evidence—mountain-building periods were short, frequent, and local.

This should have made the biology department happy, even though it promised trouble for the astronomers. Unfortunately the vertebrate fossils had produced another headache.

It had not proved difficult to set up a general sequence almost certainly corresponding to the course of evolution on the planet, spanning what must have been several hundred million years, if Earth could serve as an example. This sequence started with things just barely possessed of hard-enough interior parts to preserve, ran through bony creatures comparable to the fishes, and led eventually to legged creatures which quite obviously breathed air and spent their lives, or most of them, on dry land. It would have been nice to have been able to put the simple end of this series at the bottom of a page and Dar Lang

137

Ahn at the top, with logically intermediate forms in between, but this was rendered impossible by the fact that every fossil vertebrate found that was possessed of bony limbs at all had six of them. Dar was sufficiently human to have two arms and two legs, with no visible trace of any others.

At the biologists' urgent plea the native submitted to having a set of X-ray photographs made of himself. He was as interested as anyone in looking at the results, and was as able as any biologist to see that his skeleton bore no traces of a third pair of appendages.

Dar by now was as familiar with the general principles of evolution as the average educated human being and could see why the professionals were bothered. Even before anyone had asked he commented, "It looks as though nothing you've found in the rocks could be a direct ancestor of my race. I suppose we might have come from some other world, as Nils once thought, but there is nothing in any book I have ever read, or that any Teacher has ever told me, to suggest such a thing."

"That spikes that one," remarked the biologist sadly.

"Not entirely; it is quite possible that it happened so long ago that either we kept no records or they have been lost in the meantime. However, I'm afraid it will be a little difficult to prove."

"You're probably right. I think one thing that had better be done is to look for definitely recent formations."

The geologists had listened to this conversation; it took place during one of the regular breaks for meals. One of them now spoke up.

"It's a little hard to look at a formation casually and say, 'this is less than a million years old.' We're keeping our eyes open, of course, but you know perfectly well that dating comes afterward—after excavation, and finding fossils and comparing them with other formations."

"How about unconsolidated material on talus slopes or in caves?"

"Hardly our field, but we'll bore into any we find. I'm

not sure I recall any really well-developed cave country, though some of these limestone layers might furnish the makings if the climate cooperated."

"I have heard of caves on some of the other continents in which strange diagrams and drawings could be seen on the walls," offered Dar Lang Ahn. The party turned toward him as one.

"Can you take us there?" Several voices asked the question almost simultaneously.

"Maybe. It would be safer if we went to one of the cities on that continent and had one of the local people act as guide."

So it was arranged, after consulting with Commander Burke on the distant *Alphard*. Another flier was sent down to take the small party, so that the geologists would not be deprived of a means of travel, and several more specialists came down with the new vessel.

The continent in question lay far to the south and west of the place where the work had been going on but was still under the light of red Theer. Dar Lang Ahn found a city without difficulty and, after the usual explanations which sight of the human beings required, was able to obtain a guide. Actually, many of the citizens chose to come along to see the strangers at work; there was little of importance to be done, since all the books of this particular city had been taken to the Ice Ramparts and the people were simply awaiting death.

The caves were precisely as Dar had described; there was no doubt in the minds of any of the men that they had been inhabited by beings in the dawn of a civilization. Most of the visitors were attracted by the pictures on the walls, which Dar had mentioned, but those who knew what they were doing set to work with extreme care on the floors.

These were covered with hard-packed earth, which was carefully removed, layer by layer, and sifted for anything that might be present. The natives commented freely on everything that came to light; they had never thought of digging there themselves and apparently did not recognize any of the objects that were found. These might just as well have come from a similar cavern on Earth—tools of stone and bone and objects which might have been ornaments.

For days the digging went on. The scientists had hoped in the beginning that skeletons of the inhabitants might turn up, but they were disappointed. One of them mentioned this to Dar.

"It's not too surprising," the native answered. "I can see that these people lived in a way different from ours, but it can't have been that different. They either died at the proper time and left no trace, or died by violence, and that would hardly have happened in the caves here."

"We don't really know that it was people like yours who lived here," answered one of the scientists drily. "Somewhere in the history of this planet of yours there seems to be a big break. I might have suspected that your people came from another planet and the 'hot' ones were native to Abyormen, if we didn't know about the father-son relationship you have with them."

"Perhaps we both did," suggested Dar. The biologist brightened.

"That's a possibility. I wish the people who lived in these caves had drawn a picture or two of themselves."

"How do you know they didn't?" The scientist looked up at the weird creatures whose images sprawled across the limestone walls and ceilings.

"I don't," he said sadly. "You would bring that up. At least none of them are six-limbed, which at least *suggests* the animal life at the time this cave was inhabited was more closely related to you than what we found in the rocks can have been."

The scientist went back to his work, and Dar Lang Ahn, for the first time since Kruger had known him, went off by himself. He saw the boy looking after him and called back with his equivalent of a smile, "Don't worry, I just want to be alone for a while. I have a lot of thinking to do. Don't be afraid to call me if anything exciting happens."

Kruger felt relieved but was not quite sure what would be listed as exciting by his little friend. At first, after the arrival of the *Alphard*, virtually everything had seemed to qualify; the native had difficulty in keeping his attention on one thing at a time, since everything in his vicinity demanded examination. As time went on that tendency had disappeared. Kruger wondered whether Dar could possibly be losing the interest in the sciences which the boy had been trying to develop. He decided that the risk was slight; this work *was* getting a trifle boring, even for Kruger. It had long since passed the point where every new fossil, flint knife, or piece of limestone added noticeably to their fund of knowledge.

He wondered whether it would be worth while to return to the *Alphard* with Dar to see what the astronomers were doing. It would be a change and if Dar's interest really was flagging, unlikely as that seemed, it might take a new turn for the better. He would make the suggestion when Dar emerged from his contemplation.

It turned out that the little native was not tired of geology, however. His natural courtesy made him suggest that they go back to the other party for "just a little while" before returning to the ship; he would not have considered a return at all had he not realized that Kruger was getting bored.

The geology group, when they did get back to it, had made progress—more than they or anyone had a right to expect; so much that Kruger's boredom disappeared within seconds after landing at the current site of operations. Briefly, they had found the "break" in the geological sequence.

It had dawned on one of the scientists, after much fruitless labor, that the drastic climatic change each long year should produce an effect similar to, but more pronounced than, the seasonal changes in such formations as varved clays on Earth. Lakes, for example, should dry up completely and alternate wind-blown with water-laid sediments in a much more distinct fashion than had ever been seen on the home planet. With this thought in mind they had selected a large, shallow lake. A series of cores from the edge compared with a similar series from the deepest part of the body of water had led to results which were fairly certain to make the astronomers very happy.

The seasonal changes as described by the Teacher in the distant village of the geysers had been going on, apparently, for just a trifle under six million years according to one worker's theory, or a trifle over ten million according to another's. The two schools of thought were about evenly divided, the first basing its figures on the assumption that the long year had always had its present length of about sixty-five terrestrial years, the second insisting that the seasonal period must have been more or less steadily decreasing in length. This group had no suggestions for explaining such a phenomenon but stuck to their interpretation of the data. Dar Lang Ahn was fascinated; it was the first time that he had realized that positive knowledge did not always result at once from scientific investigation.

It remained for the leader of the party to sum up the geological situation over the first meal after Dar and Kruger had returned.

"This seems to be the story of this planet, according to present evidence," he said. "It originated about as long ago as Earth, give or take a billion years, and as far as we can tell in the same manner. It passed through the usual stage of cooling, and eventually water was able to condense. Its primary atmosphere was probably retained a trifle better than Earth's, since the velocity of escape here is over twenty per cent higher. Life started, probably spontaneously in the usual manner but possibly from adventitious spores, and developed on a path comparable to that of the other planets with which we are familiar—that is, it drastically modified the primary atmosphere until it became more or less like that of Earth.

During this period, which lasted for most of the planet's existence, the tremendous climatic changes now associated with its sun's periodic passage close to Alcyone do not seem to have been occurring; at least, no evidence whatever has been found to suggest they were, and a number of very significant facts indicate the contrary. For example, in some of the fossil beds great numbers of shell-fish and other creatures of apparently identical species but widely differing size are found, without any layering which would suggest that the smaller ones died earlier. It would seem from such facts that the life of Abyormen, at that time, was normal from our point of view in its reproductive habits—creatures were born, grew old, and died pretty much at random.

"Life evolved to the stage of air-breathing vertebrates under these conditions, the characteristic types produced all being six-limbed. There is no evidence that intelligent beings evolved.

"Then somewhere between five and ten million years ago, the tremendous temperature changes produced by Alcyone began to occur and virtually all the life of the planet was wiped out. Either a few simple forms survived and gave rise to the present species, which get around the climate situation in the way we now know, or more spores arrived, or a totally new generation of life took place.

"We still know very little about these last few million years; it seems the consensus that we should actually drain this lake and conduct major excavations in its bed to find remains of the life of this period. However, we do know that at the moment the general life of the planet exists under a form of alternating generations which enable it to survive in two widely different environments. Are there any additions or corrections to this summary?"

"Just a comment; astronomical help is urgently needed," came a voice.

"I agree. I have been recording this little speech and will send the tape up to the *Alphard* as soon as possible."

143

The meal ended with no further contributions to science.

"What do you think of it, Dar?" Kruger asked later. "Does this go very badly against what your Teachers have told you?"

"It doesn't conflict at all; they never told us anything about such possibilities. Knowing what the Teachers are, now, I can suppose that is because they never thought of them themselves."

"Isn't there some chance of your Teachers' objecting to your telling all this? Or, if they don't object, at least some of the 'hot' Teachers will."

"I've been thinking about that. I think our own Teachers will be as interested as I am, and I have come to the conclusion that all the other Teachers know about our doings is what our own report to them by radio. The others couldn't live anywhere near the Ice Ramparts."

"Not even underground?"

"A long way down, maybe, but they still couldn't watch very closely. For one thing, didn't that one at the geyser village mention that there was no way for you to see him or him to see you, since no barrier that would keep you both safe could be seen through?"

"I hadn't thought of that. But if he depends on reports from your Teachers, why couldn't they have just *said* they had killed me, instead of actually trying to carry out his orders?"

"Well, if that ever occurred to them they probably thought that the reason he wanted you killed was of such a nature that he was bound to detect the results if you weren't. If my people did learn a lot of your science right afterward, for example, it would be quite hard to hide."

"I suppose so. Still, I'd certainly take a chance rather than kill a friend."

"Perhaps they weren't sure how much of a friend you were. Remember, they hadn't been with you as long as I, and—well, you do have some rather odd characteristics,

144

you know. I can understand that 'hot' Teacher's feeling that way."

"I suppose so. We know each other pretty well now, but we still find each other queer at times. It doesn't bother me any more, though."

"Nor me." The two looked at each other with a more nearly complete understanding, in that moment, than they had ever achieved before or were to attain later.

XIII. ASTRONOMY; XENOLOGY

THE FLIER that took the geological report to the astronomers also carried Dar Lang Ahn and Nils Kruger back to the *Alphard*. Dar had followed the summary as far as it went, but he did not see just how astronomy was needed to check on the theories of the rock specialists. His curiosity about all matters allied to the physical sciences had reached a level that few human beings experience after leaving childhood.

He listened carefully as the record of the geologist's summary was played over by the astronomers, but heard nothing he did not remember from its original utterance. He listened carefully to the conversation of these new scientists and never considered that they might regard his insistent questions as a discourtesy—which, as a matter of fact, most of them did not.

"I am afraid I do not know exactly what you mean when you say that Arren may have 'captured' Theer and Abyormen," Dar would ask at one point.

"I think young Kruger explained something of Newton's laws to you," was the beginning of the answer.

"Normally, any two bodies attract each other according to definite law, and that attraction, plus the ordinary fact of inertia—the thing that keeps a stone traveling after it leaves the hand that throws it—results in definite, predictable motions of those bodies, such as the *Alphard* around your planet at this moment. By 'capture' we simply imply that originally Theer did *not* travel around Arren, but had its own path through space, and this path carried it close to Arren. The star's attractive forces changed the paths so that now they travel around each other."

"That seems clear enough. But I gathered that some of you found fault with this idea?"

"Plenty of fault. Capture doesn't ordinarily occur; it calls, as a rule, for very special circumstances."

"Why? If this force varies with distance as you say, I should think that all that would be needed would be for the two objects to get close enough together. In fact, I don't see why Theer and Arren haven't fallen into each other long ago, if what you say is right."

"Good point. The trouble is, as two objects fall toward each other their speed increases—you can see that. Unless they are aimed exactly right to start with they won't collide, and unless they collide they'll start going apart again, slowing down just as fast as they picked up speed before. The outbound path will be shaped just like the inbound one, so you won't see them spiraling together. Here, I'll show you."

Since the *Alphard* was in free fall, demonstration of the point was easy enough. Two electrically charged pith balls in the evacuated air lock behaved in a manner that made the whole affair quite clear to the curious Abyormenite.

"Then how could a capture ever take place?" he asked when his instructor had re-entered the main part of the ship and doffed his space suit. "I suppose it's possible some way or you wouldn't even have mentioned it."

"It's possible—just. If a third object is present, moving exactly the right way with respect to the others, things may turn out just right, though the probability of such an event is not awfully high; and if I'd let air into the lock a moment ago its friction would have caused the pith balls to spiral together."

"I suppose the idea is that some of the other stars in this group served as the third body."

"I hate to depend on such an idea, because they're pretty far apart, but that may account for the situation."

"At any rate it is possible that this sort of thing may account for the beginning of the hot times on Abyormen."

"Possible. I'd not like to say more." The Abyormenite had to be content with that—for the time being.

Naturally it did not take very many answers involving the terms "perhaps" and "probably" to start Dar pondering on the "how-do-you-know" type of question. Up to a point the astronomers bore with him even then, but eventually they suggested as tactfully as possible that he have Kruger teach him a little elementary algebra.

It never occurred to Dar to be hurt. He was mildly annoyed at himself for not thinking of this before, since so many of his previous questions had involved bits of mathematics in their answers. He went gaily off to find Kruger, who no longer accompanied him everywhere since his great improvement in English.

Dar failed to notice the slight dismay that his request caused his human friend; he settled down and wanted to learn algebra at once. Kruger did his best, but was not the world's best teacher. He might have done better had he not been obsessed with a fear that this sort of thing was likely to destroy Dar's interest in science.

He need not have worried. Most people who suffer in mathematics do so because they treat it as something to be memorized, and memorization held no terrors for Dar Lang Ahn. Perhaps for that reason he was extremely slow in grasping the basic idea of algebra as a problem-solving tool; he could learn all the rules but, faced with a problem, had precisely the same trouble as so many high-school freshmen. However, it was Kruger rather than Dar who eventually sought relief from this task.

Finding a new subject to interest Dar was not difficult, but for private reasons Kruger felt that it should be a non-mathematical one this time. He shared the common belief about biology's being such a subject, and decided that it was about time to find out what the life scientists had learned about Abyormen.

It turned out that this team had been trying for some time to solve the problem of examining the only 'hot' life form available—one of the Teachers in the volcano-warmed refuges. The individual at the geyser village was still not exactly cooperative, but they felt that they knew him better than any of the others; it was this being who had been selected to play host to a televison-equipped robot which the *Alphard's* engineers had improvised. Dar, seeing this device, was immediately off on a new track, and Kruger was faced with explaining television and remote control. He was still trying when everyone went aboard the landing boat with the robot.

Actually Dar felt he had a fairly clear picture of what the apparatus did, and he was beginning to get a very good idea of his chances of learning *how* it was done. He listened while Kruger talked to the Teacher on the boat's radio during the landing, but made no comments of his own.

"We would appreciate it if you would allow our robot to enter your retreat. We are sure it can stand the conditions."

"Why should I do this? What good will it do either of us?"

"You have seen us, and must have formed some of your opinions as a result. Don't you think we might modify some of our beliefs after seeing you? After all, you have claimed many times that we do not understand you, since we do not agree with your views about the spreading of knowledge. It seems to me that you would be willing to do anything which will increase our understanding."

"How do you know I have ever seen you? I told you that I knew of no substance which would keep our environments apart and which could also be seen through."

"Then you didn't tell the whole truth—you have a television device of some sort. You saw clearly enough to ask about those iron belt buckles that Dar wears."

"Very well. But how sure can I be that your seeing me will bring you strange people to your right minds?"

"I cannot tell; how can I promise what we'll conclude

from evidence we don't yet possess? In any case you can learn more of us."

"I have no particular interest in learning more about you."

"You did when you were asking me all those questions a few years back."

"I learned what I needed to know then."

"Many of the people are learning about our science, not just Dar Lang Ahn. There were scores of them watching while we investigated a cave far to the south."

"There seems little I can do to stop it."

"But if *you* will also learn from us, you could at least have some idea of what the others are finding out; and you would be able to exercise some control over what your own people learn when their time of living arrives."

Dar was a trifle confused by this argument; he did not entirely understand what the boy was trying to do and understood even less the mental operations of the distant Teacher. He did not know whether or not to be surprised when this argument seemed to convince the creature, but he could tell that Kruger was satisfied with the result.

The robot, small though it was, was too big to go through the trap at the place where Dar and Kruger had talked to the Teacher. At the latter's direction, the flier was landed near the crater in which the two travelers had been trapped for so long and the machine carried to the building in which they had found the generators. The men returned to the flier, where they all gathered around the television screen tuned to the robot's transmitter.

"What next?" one of the men asked the Teacher.

"Send your machine down the ramp." The operator complied; the little box rolled on its caterpillar treads down the slippery surface. The light grew dimmer as the bottom of the ramp was approached, and a bulb on the top of the robot was lighted to permit them to see.

"Along the corridor. Make no turns; there are other passages." The machine advanced. The corridor was long and apparently led deep into the mountain; it was some time before the way was blocked by a fairly solid door.

"Wait." They obeyed, and after a short time the door opened.

"Come quickly." The robot rolled on through and the door swung shut behind it. "Keep on; there are no more branches. I will come to meet your machine, but will travel slowly, as I have to bring my radio with me. I am still near the village."

"You need not go to the trouble of traveling unless you would rather the robot did not see that part of your station," replied one of the biologists. "The machine can make the trip without anyone's being bothered."

"Very well. I will wait here, and my companions can talk to you as well."

There must have been a single long tunnel connecting the passages under the generator building with the area under the village by the geysers. It took a long time to traverse, but eventually the robot reached a point where the corridor suddenly expanded into a large chamber about eight feet high, from which a number of other openings branched. The spokesman, who had learned enough of the Abyormenite language to be independent of Kruger or Dar most of the time, informed the Teacher of the robot's location and requested further directions.

"You are very close; it will be easier to show you the way. Wait there, and I will be with you in a moment." The men around the television screen watched intently.

In a few seconds a flicker of motion appeared in one of the openings and every eye fixed instantly on its screened image. Their attention did not waver as the newcomer walked toward the robot.

No one was particularly surprised. All except Dar had had more or less experience on Earth's exploring vessels, and had seen a wide variety of creatures turn out to be both intelligent and cultured.

This one was like nothing the Abyormenite had ever seen in his life. A melon-shaped body was supported on six limbs, so thick at the bases that they merged into each other but tapering nearly to points where they reached the floor. The human observers thought of an unusually fat-bodied starfish walking on the ends of its arms rather than spread out flat. In the light from the robot the upper third of the body appeared deep red to human eyes, with a stripe of the same color extending down to the end of each appendage; the rest was black. There were no visible eyes, ears, or similar items of equipment on the body, except for a spot at the very top which might have been anything from a closed mouth to a color peculiarity. Dar had no way of judging the size of the creature rom its televised image; the operator of the robot, judging its distance with the usual focusing lights, found that it was about Dar's height and estimated that it must weigh eighty or ninety pounds.

"I take it you see me." Dar got a distinct impression that the creature's tone was reflecting irony. There was no room for any doubt concerning this thing's identity, for the voice now coming from the robot's pick-up was the same that they had been hearing all along. "If you will have your machine follow me we will be able to relax while you find out what you wish to know." Without turning, the creature retraced its steps, and the robot followed. A short corridor led into a room about five feet high, very similar to one of those which Dar and Kruger had examined in the city. Dar watched eagerly, expecting to learn the uses of the various puzzling installations.

Some of them became obvious immediately. Three of the dome-shaped objects were occupied by creatures similar to their guide, their bodies centered on top and the six limbs draped down the side grooves. The guide himself went on to the end of the room and settled himself in one of the "wash-bowls," his limbs spread radially in all directions. It was not possible to tell from appearances that the creatures were examining the robot but there seemed little doubt that they were.

The guide, from his "couch," resumed the conversation.

"Here we are. Could you perhaps give us a more concrete idea of what you expect to learn by seeing us, and why that knowledge will make you more sympathetic with our ideas?"

"We hope to learn how you live, what you eat, what your abilities and limitations both physical and mental may be, and as much as possible about your connection with the 'cold' people who are your children and ancestors. With that knowledge, we may understand better why you object to the spread of technical knowledge on this world. At the moment I must confess that your attitude reminds us of certain historical groups on our own world, and every time in the past that such a group has managed to curtail or control the spread of knowledge the result has been extremely unfortunate. If the people of Abyormen are so different from us that this result should not be expected we'd like to know it."

"How have the people who have seen you at your work reacted to all this new information?"

"They are almost without exception interested. One at least has learned a good deal, and convinced us that your people are at least as intelligent as ours."

"I suppose you mean Dar Lang Ahn. No doubt he is planning to expand the refuges of his Teachers or construct a flying machine like yours?"

"He has made no mention of it, but you may ask him. He is here with us."

Dar was startled at this turn of the conversation, but spoke without hesitation.

"Of course I had not thought of such a thing. I have not learned enough for either task in any case."

"There is something else I trust you have not learned from these creatures, which your friend Kruger has taught me. However, what you have learned yourself will soon be of little importance."

"Of course." Dar became silent and the conversation's subject changed.

"I suppose you control this machine by some modification of radio," one of the beings on the dome-shaped "chairs" remarked. The biologist admitted that this was so. "What sort of waves do you use, that are effective through so much rock? The set with which we have been talking to you has a broadcasting antenna on the surface."

"I cannot give that information in detail myself," replied the biologist, "as it is not my field of knowledge. The robot has an antenna, but it is not very noticeable; if you examine its body closely you will find a coil of wire wound many times about the upper part, just below the turret that carries the eye." The questioner arose from his seat and walked toward the machine on all six limbs; Dar noticed that it betrayed none of the clumsiness or difficulty with motion so often showed, especially in the last few years, by his own Teachers. Arrived at the robot, the being stood on four of the legs and used the other two to grope over its surface. A bundle of small tendrils, which evidently served the purpose of fingers, became visible at the tip of each limb during this process.

"I can feel the coil," it said after a moment, "though it is too small—at least in its individual wires—to see."

"I'm afraid the light is not very well located for that purpose," replied the biologist. "We did not consider its use except for our own convenience."

"What? You mean there is a light on this machine, too? When you started to speak I thought you referred to ours. If you will bring the robot over to it perhaps I can see a little better, but I doubt it; as I said, the wires are very fine."

The biologists all saw what the trouble was, in general; the speaker said in a resigned tone, "Yes, there is a light on the robot, at the very top, a small cylinder which you can probably feel even if you can't see it. Where is the one to which you were referring?"

"There." Another limb left the floor and gestured.

Dar Lang Ahn, following the indication, saw only the pipe-and-nozzle arrangement which Kruger had described as a gas light.

"You mean that pipe?" asked the biologist. Kruger hastily explained his idea, speaking a split-second before Dar would have.

"But if it's a gas jet why isn't it lighted?" was the objection.

"Maybe it is. Maybe it's a hydrogen flame that doesn't show up in the light from our robot." Instantly the operator cut the light in question, but nothing was visible on the screen and he immediately restored it. During the brief exchange the Teacher had affirmed that the pipe in question was indeed what he meant.

"Apparently we see by different kinds of light," the biologist said. "Were you aware of that? Your 'cold' people are a little different from us in that respect, but we are nearly enough alike to use the same lighting devices, so you must differ from them, too."

"We knew that they could see smaller objects than we, but did not know the reason. We did not know that there were different kinds of light."

"You are not aware that the waves your radio uses are the same, except for length, as those used for seeing?"

"Ridiculous! Radio waves travel too rapidly for the speed to be measured, if they take any time at all for transit. The waves of sight, if they are waves, travel little faster than those of sound."

"Oh-ho-o-o." The human speaker was buried in thought for a moment. Then he asked, "Could you explain how that light of yours works?"

"It is simply a steam jet, expanding through a nozzle of a particular shape. It would be very difficult to describe the shape, at least in words that we both know."

"Never mind; you have told me enough. What I fail to understand now is how you could possibly know anything about the suns; you certainly can't 'see' them."

"Of course not; they can only be felt."

Dar Lang Ahn had been left behind some sentences before, and in hasty whispers the boy tried to explain what was going on.

"The 'hot' people don't see the way we do at all; it's even worse than the difference between you and me. We at least see by the same general kind of light—electromagnetic waves. From what this one says, they use some form of sound—very high frequency, I guess, since he said something about its traveling a little faster than 'ordinary' sound."

"But how could anyone see with sound?"

"I suppose you could see, after a fashion, with anything that traveled in a straight line, and sound will do that if nothing interferes with it. The very short sound waves—ultrasonics—are better than the ones we talk with in that respect. Of course, they wouldn't show anything that was very small; he said the wires were too fine to see, you remember."

The two brought their attention back to the radio conversation—at least, Kruger did. Dar, as usual, had something new to think about.

"You must have done some rather careful thinking yourselves to have deduced as much about this planetary system as you have," the biologist was saying, "since you can only detect objects outside Abyormen's atmosphere if they are radiating enough heat to feel."

"The picture I gave to your Nils Kruger was only one of several theories," the being replied calmly.

"It happens to be about right, as far as it goes. But if you can do that sort of thing with scientific reasoning why are you so prejudiced against it?"

"I wish you would stop reiterating that question. To answer it, however, what good does it do us? Are we any better off for knowing that Abyormen goes around Theer and Theer around Arren? I admit that sort of knowledge is harmless, since it cannot lead to dangerous activity, but it is a waste of time."

"In other words you divide scientific knowledge into two classes—useless items and dangerous ones."

"Practically. There is an occasional exception; the person who invented these lights did some good, of course. However, it is necessary to examine each new item of knowledge to make sure that it will not be dangerous."

"I begin to see your viewpoint. I take it, then, that you do not mind *our* wasting our time by finding things out about you."

"I don't care what you do with your time. Ask your question."

The scientists complied, and gradually Dar Lang Ahn began to understand the sort of beings his ancestors had been—and his children would be.

Their cities were scattered all over Abyormen, but they were invariably in volcanic areas where a few of their inhabitants could retreat underground and survive through the time of cold, so none of Dar's generation ever went near them—the fire taboo took care of that. It seemed likely, though the Teacher never admitted it in so many words, that the taboo was another example of influence of the "hot" Teachers over the "cold" ones. No such prohibition existed for the "hot" race, who lived and died where they chose; hence, metal articles such as Dar's belt buckles might be, and often were, found in or near low-temperature cities at the start of the "cold" life cycle. Like Dar's generation the others took great pains to insure the transmission of knowledge from one cycle to the next, though they depended less on books than on the memory of their Teachers. When Dar interrupted the questioning to ask why it would not be better for the knowledge to go from "hot" to "cold" and back to "hot" again, thus permitting both races to help in its development, the Teacher pointed out patiently that it would be virtually impossible to control the spread of information if this were done.

They were fairly competent electricians and excellent

civil engineers. Their chemistry seemed good, surprisingly enough to a race whose chemists depended heavily on sight. Astronomy, naturally, was almost nonexistent and the deeper branches of physics quite beyond them so far. They had radioactive elements, of course, but had not the faintest idea of the cause of their behavior.

Many of the human questions puzzled Dar, of course, and in some cases this was not due to his ignorance of human science. As nearly as he could tell, the men were trying to find out how these Teachers felt about Dar's own people—that is, whether they liked them, respected them, hated them as necessary inferiors, or simply regarded them as a minor but important nuisance. Dar remembered that one of the beings present had claimed friendship with him on the basis of blood relationship, though he could not for the life of him see how such relationship had been determined.

This question also occurred to the biologist, who had been one of those listening in during the interception of Kruger's first radio conversation with the Teacher and had later asked for a translation of it. Rather to Dar's surprise the Teacher had an answer.

"We arrange for the circumstances, or at least the location, of many of our ancestors' deaths. In a short time the people of this village will be ordered to the crater where Dar and Kruger were trapped for a time; there we can observe the death and the beginning of the new lives, and can keep track of who is who's offspring. We also arrange to die ourselves at preselected places when the cold season is about to start, and try to learn from the 'cold' Teachers the various places at which their new groups at the beginning of their time of living to catch the people are captured—they go out into the wilds in hunting new people, who are nothing more than wild animals at the time."

"I should think they would miss some."

"They do, as nearly as we can tell. Every now and then

158

a member of our race turns up, or sometimes even a small group of them, whose parent must have survived the whole cold season as a wild animal; at least, we have no record of him."

"Don't you know how many children a given person will have?"

"It is quite impossible to tell, depending on things such as his individual weight."

"But that doesn't seem to vary much."

"During normal life, no, but at the time of dying one may have gone for very long periods without food, or on the other hand have eaten very heavily and very recently —all according to the opportunities. Also it is impossible to tell whether any of the young children have been eaten by wild animals before they are caught, in the case of Dar Lang Ahn's people, since they do not take proper care of them as we do."

"I see." So did Dar. Good though his memory was it contained little of his brief existence before being "caught," but what little there was fitted in with what the Teacher said. He wondered why his own Teachers did not take precautions like those—and then realized that they had no chance; either the "hot" people would have to cooperate, which they seemed unwilling to do, or his own race would have to keep a group of the others under control during the hot period, as this creature did with his villagers during the cold. This seemed difficult, to put it mildly; the other race had got far enough ahead technically to have pretty complete control of the situation. Dar began to suspect strongly that this Teacher had not been frank; there were reasons other than his personal disapproval of science behind his objections to the introduction of human knowledge.

That thought grew in his mind as the conversation went on, and gave birth to others. It was Dar Lang Ahn, after the robot had started back to the flier, who made the suggestion that some of the other Teachers in their volcanically warmed retreats be contacted and questioned; and even Kruger, who knew him better than any other human being ever would, did not realize just what he was trying to find out.

XIV. BIOLOGY; SOCIOLOGY

AGAIN AND again Abyormen swung around its almost cometary orbit, and closer and closer Theer drew to its blazing primary. Abyormen, very slowly, grew hotter. To its natives this was a matter of little moment; the temperature had not yet reached the value which would activate the bacteria whose life processes would load the atmosphere with oxides of nitrogen. Until that happened Dar's people cared little whether the oceans of their planet were freezing or boiling.

The temperature did not bother the human scientists, either. Most of them had from the beginning been wearing complex protective garments which virtually air-conditioned them. Nevertheless they knew that more protection would be needed soon. Experiments with the native life, using not only bacteria but animals and plants large enough to be observed directly, had told them what to expect.

Kruger was more than satisfied with the situation. His friend had evidently become completely absorbed in the business of acquiring knowledge from the human visitors. Kruger could not always keep up with him, but the boy no longer cared much about that. If anything was certain, it was that Dar Lang Ahn had already collected far too much information to relay it all to his Teachers before the end of his normal life span. There would be no alternative to his remaining in the shelter under the ice cap when it was sealed, which meant that he would automatically become a Teacher himself.

Once or twice the boy's conscience bothered him a trifle; he wondered whether it would not have been fairer to point out to Dar what all this time spent with the human visitors must necessarily entail. Each time he thought of this, however, he managed to convince himself that the native was old enough to know what he was doing.

It might have helped had he brought the matter up, just the same.

While the human scientists could, of course, work even in the hot season of Abyormen, action would be much more awkward. Therefore they were trying to get their basic information before the change occurred. Dar watched everything that went on, as far as possible; Kruger was much less enthusiastic after seeing one of the biological tests.

This occurred after the chain-reaction effect of heat on the local bacteria had been discovered. A soil sample from the planet had been used to cover the floor of an airtight cage, and several small animals of the sort Dar and Kruger had encountered in the crater had been introduced. Several native plants were growing there as well; the biologists had tried to reproduce the planet's environment in miniature. This done, they proceeded to raise the temperature—gradually, to minimize the chance of thermal shock's complicating the situation.

The cage was well enough insulated to prevent steam from condensing on the walls, so it was still possible to see what went on within. Some water, of course, was still liquid, since the boiling of the rest had raised the pressure considerably; and quite suddenly a meter began to climb from the zero position.

It was simply a galvanometer, but it was mounted in series with a resistor consisting of a tiny, open vial of water inside the cage. The resistance of the liquid was dropping, and no one present doubted the cause. In a few seconds this became evident even to the naked eye, as the atmosphere within the cage took on a faint but unmistakable reddish-brown tint. The bacteria were at work; oxides of nitrogen were forming, acidifying any water that might still be present in liquid form—and doing something much more drastic to the life in the cage.

The animals had stopped moving, except for an uneasy turning of their heads. Each had drawn a little way from his neighbor, and stopped nibbling on the plants. For several seconds subjects and experimenters alike remained motionless while the suspense mounted.

Then the largest of the little creatures abruptly collapsed, and within the next thirty seconds the others had followed suit. Kruger stole a sidelong glance at Dar, but his little friend did not notice. He had both eyes fixed on the cage. The boy looked back at the animals, and suddenly felt sick. The tiny creatures were losing shape, melting into featureless puddles of protoplasm. The pools remained separate, even where two of the creatures had collapsed quite close together. A faint stirring motion became visible in the mounds of still-living jelly, and as he saw this Kruger's stomach failed him. He raced for the outdoors.

Dar did not seem affected; he remained for the next half hour, which was about the time it took the last of the pools to organize itself into about fifty tiny worm-like things which bore no resemblance whatever to the animal from whose body material they had been formed. These were crawling about the cage, apparently perfectly able to take care of themselves.

The plants had changed also, though not by the same process. The leaves of the larger ones dropped away and the trunks shriveled slightly. At first the watchers had supposed that the growths were simply being killed by the heat, but this hypothesis was eliminated by the appearance of hundreds of tiny knoblike excrescences on the withered trunks. These swelled slowly, apparently at the expense of the parent plant, and finally fell free in a rain of spheres which lasted several minutes.

Smaller, grasslike plants had simply withered, but other things were rapidly sprouting in their places. Less than an hour was required to transform the cage from a

163

respectable representation of the landscape outside the flier to something utterly alien to all of the watchers— Dar Lang Ahn included.

"So that's the story!" one of the biologists breathed at last. Neither he nor any of his colleagues had been affected by the sight as Kruger had been. Of course, none of them had the same personal feeling about Dar. "I suppose we should have expected quite a lot of off-spring from each individual, if this is their only means of reproduction. The population of this planet must be something terrific right after the season change."

One of the other biologists shook his head negatively.

"That part is all right," he said, "but something else isn't. Right now we're just *before* one of the changes, and there are still plenty of animals around—carnivores as well as plant eaters—and the vegetation doesn't look particularly moth-eaten. I'm afraid I can't quite believe that there's no other method of reproduction here."

"Wouldn't the need for that depend on the length of time between seasons? If this ratio is the usual one it simply means that about one individual out of fifty lives through the season."

"Right, and the season now ending lasts about forty Earth years. I refuse to believe that such a large proportion of survivors could be expected in any wild animal over such a period. We know that they eat about as much, compared to their weights, as similar animals on Earth. How about it, Dar? Don't new animals get started at various times during your life span?"

"Certainly," replied the native. "Any part of an animal will grow a whole new one, provided it is big enough. The animals we use for food certainly do that, anyway; we always leave some of the creature, for that purpose. Isn't it that way with your animals?"

"Hmph. There are some creatures on Earth capable of that sort of thing, but they're fairly primitive forms. I don't see how anything on this planet could get killed."

"Well, some animals don't leave enough of their prey

164

to grow again, of course. Then there are always things like starvation or drowning, though starvation takes a long time to shrink anything down to the point where it can't live."

One of the scientists looked thoughtfully at his own right hand, on which two fingers were represented by stumps—the relic of a childhood accident. "I suppose, Dar, that it would be foolish to ask whether your own race shares this ability of regeneration."

"I do not see why it is foolish. Yes, we have it; though in a civilized community there is, of course, very seldom any need for it. Occasionally a victim of a glider crash or something of that sort will have to replace an arm or leg."

"Or head?"

"That is a special case. If the injury is one that interrupts the regular life processes the tissues go back to the 'beginning' and reorganize to a completely new individual—or to several. As far as the original individual is concerned death has occurred. As I said, this sort of thing happens rarely."

It rather surprised the biologists, that an explanation to the phenomenon was found. However, several weeks' work with all the facilities the *Alphard* had to offer did give a reasonable answer. Richter, head of the biological crew, was glad of the chance to explain it to Commander Burke. That officer had come to question him specifically on such matters; he was worried.

"I'm bothered a trifle about these people, Richter," Burke opened the conversation. "As you know, every ship commander that goes out from Earth gets a long briefing about the risk of introducing new species in any environment. They tell us about rabbits in Australia and Japanese beetles in North America, until we get sick of the whole business of ecology. It seems to me that we've run into something that might possibly be a serious competitor for humanity, if what I've been told about Dar Lang Ahn's people is correct."

"I suppose you've read our summary about regeneration. I admit that these people are rather remarkable in some respects, but I shouldn't say they constituted any sort of danger."

"Why not? Don't they fit right into the picture—a creature entering a new environment, where its natural enemies are absent, and multiplying unchecked? These beings would swamp men out in a few years."

"I can't see it. Dar's people have the same natural enemies as men—any sort of meat-eating animal, as well as their usual diseases. They do have sickness, according to Dar. Anything like that would come with them."

"But the primary killing agent that affects the race is heat. What's going to happen if they get established on Earth, or Thanno, or Hekla, or any of a score of other worlds you and I could name? They'd be virtually immortal."

"Granting that they need heat to die 'normally,' I think you're forgetting something. They also need it to reproduce."

"Either that, or dismemberment. What happened in the Chesapeake in the days when the oystermen thought they could get rid of starfish by chopping them up and throwing them back in the water?"

"You miss the point, Commander—and I'm afraid young Kruger has missed it, too. The really important fact is that *Dar Lang Ahn's people have to die in order to reproduce.* Have you thought of it that way?" There was a long silence before the commander answered.

"No, I can't say that I have. That does put another color to the whole situation." He paused again in thought. "Have you any idea of why this occurs—or rather, since it's an obvious evolutionary development for a planet like this, *how* it occurs?"

"We have. It was hard to figure, mostly because there is a good deal of evidence that this drastic climate change only started to occur in the last ten million years or so, but a certain organism of our own planet gave us the lead."

"What? What creature of Earth is exposed to anything like the conditions met with here?"

"None, so far as I know; that wasn't the sort of lead. One of the men—Ellerbee, as I recall—was working with a group of 'hot' animals that we'd obtained in the usual way, in one of our biggest conditioned cages. He was trying to determine whether the carnivores usually left enough of their victims to reproduce, and incidentally to see the regeneration process which Dar had told us about—we didn't really know whether it applied to the 'hot' forms or not. Naturally Ellerbee was doing his best to keep track of the types and numbers of animals present, and he was a bit surprised, after a while, to find some creatures he hadn't seen before. Fortunately he didn't simply write the matter off as a slip in his earlier observations; he checked it carefully, and found that when the atmosphere and temperature change occurred it was possible to get animals from soil samples in which no 'parents' had been present."

"Which means?"

"That some of the 'hot' forms reproduce by some form of microscopic spore which survives in the soil during the unfavorable season. Whether any of the 'cold' ones can do the same is still uncertain; we haven't found any."

"And what does this imply?"

"It got Ellerbee suspicious of the general theory that Dar Lang Ahn and those fire-blooded starfish are actually alternate generations of the same species. We talked over the matter at one of our regular discussion sessions and found that there was already some more evidence in. Dan Leclos had found in one type of animal a number of small, bony spheroids which experiment had showed to be the source of the 'hot' generation for that particular species. If they were removed before exposing the creature to heat and nitrogen dioxide no descendants appeared, although the flesh behaved in the usual manner, while if the spheres themselves were exposed to the changed conditions they produced embryonic specimens of 'hot' life."

"I don't see what all that means."

"It seems to mean that the 'hot' and 'cold' forms are completely alien types of life, which originally evolved independently. Each produced spores, or some equivalent, that were capable of surviving the unsuitable conditions.

"In the natural course of evolution some of them developed the trick of attaching or implanting their spores in the bodies of active animals of the other type—perhaps by arranging for them to be eaten, as some parasites on Earth still do."

"But in that case you should be able to find the seeds, or whatever they are, in any of the creatures you examine. You said they were present in only one. How about that?"

"That's where the lead from Earth came in. You may know that there are some types of virus whose natural prey are bacteria. The virus makes contact with the germ, penetrates its cell wall, and after a while a hundred or so new viruses emerge from the deflated remains of the bacterium."

"I didn't know that, but there seems nothing strange about it."

"There isn't, so far. However, it sometimes happens that after the virus enters the body of its victim the latter goes on living as though nothing had happened."

"Still reasonable. There's always a scattering of immunes in any population."

"Let me finish. The bacterium lives out its time and divides in the usual fashion; its descendants do the same for ten or twenty or perhaps a hundred generations. Then, under the stimulus of radiation or chemicals or for no apparent reason at all most or all of the descendants of the original bacterium collapse—and clouds of virus particles emerge from the remains!"

"Eh?"

"Precisely. The original virus infected its first victim, all right, *in such a way that the reproductive material of the virus was divided when that of the bacterium did the same* and carried on to all the descendants of that first one. Eventually some change in conditions made them revert to their usual method of reproduction."

"I see," Burke said slowly. "You think that a similar ability has developed here—that every cell of a being like Dar Lang Ahn has in its nucleus the factors which will produce one of those starfish under the proper conditions."

"Exactly, and yet the relationship is no more a parent-and-child one than that between Jack Cardigan and his pet canary. There's a suspicion that the chloroplasts in earthly plants bear the same relation to them."

"I don't see what difference it makes, really."

"In a way, it might justify the attitude of the 'hot' creatures toward Dar's people."

"Perhaps. However, nothing you've said eases my first worry, except your point that both forms have to die to reproduce. You've added one thing that bothers me more."

"What's that?"

"This business about the time in which adaptation to this climate has taken place. If you're right, one at least of these races has evolved from a standing start to intelligence comparable with our own in something under ten million years. It took Earth a hundred times as long to do the job—maybe twice that. These things must be among the most adaptable life forms in the universe—and that's the point where man has held the edge, so far."

"You're afraid, I take it, that if they get access to human technology they'll spread out into the galaxy and start supplanting man?"

"Frankly, yes."

"Just where would you expect them to settle?"

"For Heaven's sake, man—anywhere! Earth—Mars—Mercury—any of fifty worlds where we can live, and as many more where we can't! If they can't stand them now they soon will—it's that adaptability that has me worried. If we get into an argument with them how do we fight—how do you kill a creature that grows new arms and legs to replace the old, that produces a whole crop of descendants if you blow it to pieces with a bomb?"

"I don't know and I don't think it matters."

"Why not?" Burke's voice sounded almost strangled by his emotion.

"Because, while Dar Lang Ahn could live on Earth and a lot of other worlds, and his fire-blooded opposite numbers could do the same in a higher temperature range, as you justly point out, none of the planets you mentioned provides *both* temperature ranges. If a group of Dar's people decides to migrate to Earth how will the 'hot' folks *whose relatives are riding along with them* like it? Dar undoubtedly wants descendants as much as one of us; how will he feel at the thought of the starfish which develop from his body moving to Vega Two, or Mercury? What happens to his kids, then? No, Commander, I realize that most of us have decided, pretty much without discussion, that the Teacher down there by the hot springs is an opinionated, narrow-minded, dictatorial old fuddy-duddy whose opinion isn't worth the energy used to express it, but if you'll think a bit longer you'll realize that he's more far-sighted than a lot of others I could name!"

Burke shook his head slowly, keeping his gaze fixed on the biologist.

"I had thought of that point long ago, Dr. Richter, and I suppose you're right in thinking that that Teacher has done the same. I'm a little disappointed, however, that you have gone no farther."

"How's that?"

"Your point is well taken—only if these races lack

technical knowledge! Dar won't mind having the gene structures which are to produce his offspring spend a few years anywhere the starfish carrying them wants to—if he knows that eventually that creature will either travel to a planet where they can develop or park himself in a mechanical refrigerator to achieve the same end. Remember, those creatures will have the same desires as regards offspring, and they will have to cooperate with Dar's race to satisfy them. If the natives of this planet get off it, on the basis of knowledge they've either picked up from us or acquired themselves, there's going to be one of the most cooperative teams in history spreading through the star clouds—and man is going to take a back seat, if he survives at all."

"It seems to me that that very cooperation would be a good example to the rest of us, if it happens. These races certainly aren't very close to such a relationship right now."

"No, and it's to our interest to see that they never get there. I don't like to do it any better than you do, or than young Kruger will, but I'm afraid the only thing we can reasonably do is prevent Dar Lang Ahn from taking the knowledge he has acquired back to his people. Unless we do that we've given them the galaxy."

"You're right—I don't like it. How can we justify such a thing, after we ourselves have encouraged him to learn all he could?"

"We can't justify it," Burke said grimly, "but we're going to do it. Sure, I'll hate myself for the rest of my life, but in my considered judgment it is best for the human race that Dar Lang Ahn should not see his own people again."

"I'm afraid you're right, though it doesn't make me any happier."

"Nor me. Well, in common fairness we'd better tell him now. I'll call a meeting of the entire group and let anyone with any other helpful data present it. That's about as fair as I can be."

"Young Kruger may not have data, but he'll have objections."

"I realize that. He doesn't know what a favor I'll be doing him." The biologist looked sharply at the old officer, but Burke had nothing more to say.

XV. ASTRONOMY; LOGIC

DAR LANG AHN heard the biological report with only his usual interest, since such phrases as fluorinated hydrocarbons and silicones still meant very little to him. He did react, however, to Commander Burke's announcement, and the reaction was not a mild one.

Devastating though his emotion was it did not become vocal, for Nils Kruger started talking first. Dar listened to precisely the points about fair play, honesty, and decency that had been discussed by Burke and Richter, but did not fully understand the terms used. In any case he did not pay full attention; he was trying to decide on his own line of action.

Argument would presumably be useless. The men would have formed their opinions on what they had learned of him and his people. He could not quite see why Abyormen constituted a danger to the galaxy, but had come to hold the opinions of the human scientists in high respect. In spite of this he found that his natural sense of duty was urging him to go against Burke's decision—to argue, lie, or commit violence to get what he considered vital information back to his own people. A third impulse was furnished by his natural curiosity; had it not been for duty, he would have liked nothing better than traveling to Earth with his friends—if he could still call them that—and seeing some of the worlds Kruger and the astronomers had described to him. He might have started to speak, bringing his dilemma out in the open, but Kruger never gave him a chance. The boy was forgetting all the discipline that cadet training had drilled into him and coming perilously close to using personal abuse on the commander. The full significance of this escaped Dar, of course, since he had only the vaguest knowledge of Kruger's background, but he did understand clearly that the boy wanted to let him go back to his people.

It seemed unlikely that Kruger would win his argument with the commander; Dar did have some idea of the relative ranks involved. Could he slip out while the argument was going on and steal one of the landing boats? He had watched carefully more than once while they were being flown; could he handle one himself? With his memory there was no question of his pushing the wrong button after he had once seen the right one pushed. However, his lifetime of flying preserved him from what would almost certainly have been a fatal error. He realized that there was much more to handling any sort of space ship than he could possibly have learned by observation alone in a couple of dozen rides.

Could he stow away? Unlikely. These men, whatever else they might be, could not be called stupid. Once the commander had ordered that Dar Lang Ahn was not to return to Abyormen, steps would most certainly be taken to enforce the decision.

Could Kruger steal a boat and fly him down? Undoubtedly he could, since he could certainly fly the machines, but Dar was hampered in deciding the answer to this question by his ignorance of the weight of authority among human beings. There was no way to tell whether the boy *would*. He recognized this lack, and filed the idea for future checking when he could see Kruger alone.

Could he—

His reverie was interrupted at this point by the raised voice of Commander Burke.

"Mr. Kruger! I called this meeting for intelligent discussion, not tear-jerking or personal abuse. Unless you have a meaningful argument to present, you will be silent. I understand your feelings, I share them, and I have weighed the moral issues involved at least as carefully as you have. Do me the favor to remember that I have a number of responsibilities which you do not as yet share and which you quite evidently have not considered. I did not ask for a vote or an expression of opinion from anyone. I stated a conclusion I have reached, to wit, that Dar Lang Ahn's race—or races, I suppose I should say—will constitute a danger to mankind if they leave their native planet. I firmly believe that the government will share that opinion. However, if you or anyone else has *information* which might require the modification of it, by all means speak up."

Kruger was silent, realizing suddenly just how far he had gone and feeling gratitude to the officer for the relative mildness of the rebuke. Unfortunately he had nothing to say which could possibly be construed as information.

The silence was interrupted by another of Dar's friends, an astronomer named Murchison.

"I'm afraid that there is another point to be considered," he said slowly, "and I'm fairly sure it will not only cause the government to reach a different conclusion from yours, Commander, but will have them doing their level best to get both Abyormenite races educated as soon as possible."

"Let's have it!" the commander replied instantly.

"The main fact is that if we leave these people on this planet, it will amount to an act of genocide. This planet is a poor home for us and at the moment a necessary home for its inhabitants, but before too long it's not going to be any sort of home for anyone."

"How long? And why not?"

"Because this is not a stable system. Abyormen seems to have been formed in a more or less normal manner as a planet of the red dwarf sun the local natives call Theer, but at that time Alcyone was nowhere in the neighborhood. For one thing the light pressure of Alcyone is such that a planet could not have formed in its neighborhood."

"I've heard that before, but didn't see how you were going to keep that theory going, since the planet is here."

"I didn't for a while myself. However, there is geological evidence that what I say is true; the tremendous seasonal changes of this planet, due to the elliptical path of Theer about Alcyone, did not occur throughout the early portion of the world's history, but only in the last few million years. One of two things happened; either Theer was captured by Alcyone fairly recently, or the giant star actually formed in the neighborhood of the dwarf. I incline to the latter view; we are inside a star cluster where the space is loaded—relatively speaking—with gas and dust. It is more than likely that Theer's entrance into the cluster, if it was not originally a member of it, created enough turbulence to start a condensation in its neighborhood."

"I can see how that fits in with the geological time scale, but doesn't it emphasize my point about the adaptability of these races?"

"In a way, yes, but I don't believe that any organic structure could adapt to the fate in store for this system. Remember what I said—the space in this vicinity is full of gas and dust. Therefore, it is not a frictionless medium. That is why the alternate theory—that Alcyone captured the Theer system—is possible. The friction is continually shortening Theer's orbit. More and more of each year is being spent in the hot zone, and less and less at a distance from the giant star which permits Dar's people to live. Unless Alcyone drifts out of the Pleiades cluster, which it doesn't seem about to do, another half million or million years will see the red sun, together with Abyormen, dropping into it."

"That's a long time."

"It's an indefinite time, and long before it expires Abyormen will be uninhabitable for even the 'hot' form of life. It's our business to get these races off the planet or at least help them get themselves off; otherwise we're guilty of criminal negligence."

176

"But if Alcyone's light pressure kept the matter which should have formed planets away from it, how can there be enough in the vicinity to create the friction you say?"

"The effect of light pressure on a particle, compared to that of gravity, is a function of the size and density of the particle. I assure you that we have made plenty of measurements throughout this volume of space and I'm not just guessing at what will happen. The only thing I'm seriously doubtful about is whether Theer itself will pick up enough matter so that its own increasing luminosity will sterilize this planet before the final fall occurs. I can't say which will happen first, but one of them will most certainly happen."

"But where could we take these people? I doubt that there's a planet in the galaxy duplicating this seasonal situation."

"I'd be willing to bet that there are thousands. I admit we haven't found them yet, but there's a lot of galaxy still unexplored. Even if there aren't any they could learn to live in ships—might even get along better that way, with numerous members of both races alive at once. I can see a ship with one portion hot and one cold, with people living in both parts and moving from one to the other when their lives reach the appropriate stage. That situation will certainly be better for the Abyormenites than settling on any Earth-type planet would be—and I'm sure the government will see it the same way. We'll be back here setting up technical schools before you're an admiral, Commander—setting them up for the both races. I don't care what the present crop of 'hot' Teachers may think; a bit of astronomy will change their minds."

"If you can teach any astronomy to a race that sees by means of sound waves," Burke pointed out drily. "However, that's a quibble. I agree with you." Kruger's face showed his relief; no face could have shown what Dar felt. "Dar Lang Ahn may continue learning from our scientists as long as he sees fit, and return to his own people with his information as soon as he wishes. In a way

177

I am taking a slight chance in permitting this, but I have no serious doubt as to the official decision. Young fellow," he turned abruptly to Kruger, "this is an excellent example of the risk of reaching a decision on the basis of insufficient evidence. Just don't let it impress you too much. You never will get *all* the data bearing on any question, and you'll have to come up with an answer sometime—particularly if you are commanding any sort of space flier. You'll have to learn to accept the risk of making a premature judgment. If it kills you some time, don't let me hear you complain."

"No, sir," replied Kruger.

"Very well. Dar, I will not apologize for my previously announced policy. However, I will give you any assistance you may need while you are still with us, provided it lies within my power."

"Thank you, Commander. My Teachers will appreciate your action."

"Isn't it pretty nearly time for your refuge to be sealed?"

"One more year. I should return as soon as you will allow, however, since there is much for me to report."

"We will take you down as soon as possible. Mr. Kruger, I assume you will want to go with him. I will handle the flier; anyone else whose duties permit may come along, up to the capacity of the boat. We will stay down until the shelter is sealed, so anyone who wants to observe that operation can plan on a three-week stay away from the *Alphard*. The boat will depart in twenty hours, which should give anyone who wants to take apparatus plenty of time to get it aboard.

"Dar Lang Ahn, do you suppose your Teachers could find a use for a radio which does not operate on the same sort of wave as those of your fiery friends—one on which you could talk to us without their knowledge, if you wished?" Kruger restrained a grin with difficulty; the old coot was human, in spite of his devotion to duty.

"Such a device would quite possibly be of use, Commander. We would appreciate it very much."

"All right, we'll see that a few of them are aboard the boat. Meeting adjourned."

The approach to the landing platform at the Ice Ramparts was rather different this time. The space flier, supported and guided by fields similar to those which hurled the *Alphard* through interstellar space with total indifference to the law of the speed of light, did not have the maneuvering limitations of the gliders. This was just as well, for the platform was crowded with the aircraft in a way that might have made a landing difficult even for Dar Lang Ahn. For the first time Kruger saw Teachers on the surface, sometimes directing activities and sometimes simply watching.

The approach of the boat was noted, and a group of natives gestured toward one side of the platform, where gliders were being pulled aside to make a cleared space.

The instant the air lock of the little ship opened Dar and Kruger were outside, both burdened with the radio equipment Burke had donated. The native led the way into the tunnels and they started the long, long walk to the main body of the refuge located so far under the ice cap. Kruger no longer wondered at the reason for the location; he was still somewhat surprised that these people had been able to build it.

The whole place seemed far more active than it had been before, with scores and even hundred of the little natives scurrying about on their mysterious errands.

"There must be a lot of library work to be done," Kruger remarked as he gestured at one of these groups.

"The books should all have come in long ago," Dar replied. "The problem now is food. Normally, there is enough on hand many years before the time comes, but no chances are taken. We keep bringing it in until the last possible moment."

"What are you going to do?"

"Get together any Teachers who can devote their time

to me and start reporting. There should be a number available, as they know that I am coming with knowledge."

"I expect that reporting will keep you pretty busy from now on."

"Yes, Nils. I suppose you would like to see this place once more as it is prepared for the time of dying, but I will not be free to act as your guide. No doubt some one will be found who can help you, though."

Kruger stopped and laid a hand on the little native's shoulder.

"You'll not let the doors close without seeing me again, will you?" he asked. "I don't want to interfere with the work that has to be done, but I don't want to see the last of you—at least, for a good many of my years —this soon."

Both eyes swerved up and took in Kruger's anxious face for a moment.

"I will see you again before the Ramparts are sealed. I promise it," said Dar Lang Ahn. They resumed the journey, the boy satisfied.

Dar's prediction that a committee would be awaiting him proved correct. It was composed, the boy noticed, of beings of his own stature—the new Teachers. One of the giants he had met before, however, offered to act as his guide, and under the tall being's leadership Kruger saw the now completely organized libraries, the food-storage bins in the upper levels only a few feet from the overlying ice, and great beds in the warmer lower levels where plants similar to terrestrial fungi grew.

At length, he was led upward to the landing platform, where activity continued undiminished. Gliders lunged into the sky, bound for the distant cities and, if there was time after they arrived, another load of food. Others landed, in the relatively small space left for that purpose; busy ground crews were constantly dragging gliders either to one side of the platform or into the cavern to make room for the newcomers.

"Aren't I taking up a lot of your time?" Kruger asked when they reached the surface. "This seems to be the busiest time of life for your people."

"There is nothing more for me to do," was the answer. "My successor has taken over."

"But don't you stay in the Ramparts this time?"

"No. My life is done. A few of us will stay to make sure that the seals are properly in place, but that is not one of my tasks. As soon as I can be of no more use to you I will leave."

"But I thought they had dismantled all the gliders capable of carrying you."

"They have. I will leave on foot. We do not return to the cities."

"You mean—" Kruger stopped; he knew that Dar had told his people very little over the radio, and was not sure how much this being knew. The Teacher either knew or guessed what was in his mind, however.

"No, we do not return to the cities. It is not the custom; has not been for so long that I can no longer give you the precise details of the reason. However, it is better that we meet our ends where the heat is not very great—at least, not before our bodies are destroyed in other ways. When you no longer need me, I will—take a walk on the ice cap."

Kruger found himself with nothing to say, except that he still felt the need of the Teacher's company. At his invitation the being entered the flier and was met with great interest by the biologists who had come down. One of these spoke enough of the native language to render the boy's presence unnecessary and he returned to the landing platform to watch for Dar. However, his little friend did not appear and the endless activity kept Nils's attention until he found it necessary to sleep.

So the time passed. Gradually the number of gliders diminished, as the arrivals ceased and those already present headed for the other hemisphere. The sight of the casual way in which these beings started their last flights was depressing, not only to Kruger but to the other human beings watching.

"I guess it's just the way you're brought up," one of the men remarked, "but if I knew I had a week to live I'd look a good deal soberer."

"I think it's more like three weeks," said Kruger. "They seal this place a year in advance of the expected atmosphere change, just to play safe."

"Don't quibble."

"I didn't mean to. I got the impression from Dar, though, that he felt sorry for us—living from day to day without knowing when the end was to come. I suppose it's just as hard for him to realize that we're used to it, as it is for us to picture his attitude."

"That's true." It was a new voice that made this answer, and Kruger turned to see Commander Burke standing in the air lock. "I should have liked to know your friend better, Mr. Kruger, but I don't suppose we'd ever really *know* him—not even you."

"Maybe not, sir, but I can't help feeling that I do."

"Good luck to you. Isn't it nearly time for this sealing ceremony to take place?" Several more men were emerging from the little ship.

"I haven't kept close track, sir, but I guess it must be, at that. Nearly all the gliders are gone, and—and I've seen a number of the big Teachers leaving the platform and starting around the mountain." His voice shook a little as he mentioned this and the commander nodded gravely.

"Yes. The one who acted as your guide went the last time you were asleep."

"What? I didn't know that, sir."

"I know you didn't. It was by my advice that he went then. I thought it was better that way." Something in the tone of the officer's voice forbade further questioning.

Several more of the giant Teachers appeared on the platform at this point and the men stopped their conversation to watch them. One approached the group by the air lock and spoke.

"We are about to check the sealing of the outer gates. These are located some distance down the tunnel, as we have found it desirable to let ice come into the upper caverns later in the hot season. Would you care to come with us, to watch the operation?"

"Wait a minute! Dar Lang Ahn promised he'd see me before the doors were closed! Where is he?"

"He is coming. If you come with us you should meet him in the tunnel. I see his glider is waiting." The being turned without further remark and the men followed, Burke watching the dazed Kruger with something like pity showing on his face.

The doors were about three hundred yards down the tunnel and, true to the Teacher's prediction, Dar Lang Ahn was waiting beside them.

"Hi, Nils!" he called as the boy came in sight. "Sorry I was so long. There was a lot to do, believe me!"

"Dar! You can't have finished—but this Teacher said—"

"Sure I did. Had to. Come on up to the surface—I want to check my glider. Or would you rather watch them seal the door?"

"But they can't seal it yet! You can't possibly have told them all you learned from us! You've got to stay and be a Teacher for the next generation!" The little native was silent for a moment, then spoke in a softer voice.

"Come with me, Nils. Maybe I did something I shouldn't have, but it's done. I'll try to explain to you." He gestured along the tunnel and the boy obeyed silently, staring at his little friend. Dar started talking as they went; the commander looked after them, shaking his head.

"Nils, I couldn't do it. I thought about the point you've just mentioned and when I first started to learn things from you I rather planned to do what you've just suggested. I didn't like it, of course, but it seemed to be my duty. Then I stayed with you and your people and—

kept learning. Astronomy, geology, biology, archaelogy, mathematics, and all the other specialties that the men of your group represent. There was just too much of it."

"Too much for *you* to remember?" Kruger stopped, his surprise momentarily covering his grief.

"Not too much to remember, no, but too much to grasp properly. I could have stayed down below and dictated scores of books about everything I had seen you do or heard you say, but even though I understood a good deal of it my people wouldn't. There was something else they needed more, and gradually I came to understand what it was.

"It's *method*, Nils. It's the very way you people go about solving problems—imagination and experiment together. That was the thing my people had to learn and the thing I had to show them. Their problems are different from yours, after all; they'll have to solve them for themselves. Of course, the facts are important, too, but I didn't give too many of those. Just scattered pieces of information here and there, so that they could check their answers once in a while."

"Then—then it was my own fault you're doing this! I deliberately exposed you to as many different fields of knowledge as I could, so there'd be no chance of your getting it all recorded before the time of dying!"

"No! It's not your fault, if you can call it a fault at all. You showed, indirectly I admit, just what we need to know. I was looking for an excuse to avoid staying in the Ramparts; if you want to say you furnished it, all right —and thanks." He paused; they had reached the platform and Dar began without preamble to make sure his glider was ready for launching.

"But—can't you come with us, instead? You don't have to go back to Kwarr and—and—" Kruger could not finish the sentence. Dar straightened from his task and looked at him narrowly. For a moment or two he seemed to struggle with some decision; then he shook his head in the negative gesture he had learned from Kruger.

"I'm afraid not. I think I see a little of how you feel, friend Nils, and in a way I am sorry to leave you behind, but—would *you* come with *me?*" He almost gave his equivalent of a smile as he asked this. Kruger was silent.

"Of course you wouldn't—you couldn't. You expect to live a long time yet, even though you don't know how long." He gripped one of Kruger's hands with his small claw. "Nils, many of your years from now there will be quite a lot of my people who are part of me. I will be gone, but you may still be around. Maybe with what you and I have done for them some of those people will be scientists, and will have learned to get respect instead of contempt from the 'hot' ones, and to start something which may in time be a civilization like yours. I would like to think that you will be helping them."

He vaulted into the seat of the glider and, without giving the boy time to say a word, tripped the catapult.

Kruger watched the little aircraft out of sight. It did not take long to vanish, for his eyes were not as clear as they should have been, but he was still facing the direction in which it had gone when he finally muttered, "I will be!" He turned away as the thud of a great door sounded from the tunnel.

IN FANTASY AND SCIENCE FICTION
BALLANTINE BOOKS
BRINGS YOU THE BEST

Piers Anthony	*Chthon* *Omnivore*
Dave Van Arnam	*Starmind*
John Brunner	*The Whole Man* *The Squares Of The City* *Double, Double* *Stand On Zanzibar*
John Heyden Howard	*The Eskimo Invasion*
Anne McCaffrey	*Restoree* *Dragonflight*
Larry Niven	*World Of Ptaavs* *Neutron Star* *A Gift From Earth*
John Norman	*Tarnsman Of Gor* *Outlaw Of Gor* *Priest-Kings Of Gor* *Nomads Of Gor*
Fred Saberhagen	*Berserker* *Brother Assassin*
Robert Silverberg	*Thorns* *The Masks Of Time* *Up The Line*
William Tenn	*Of Men And Monsters* *The Square Root Of Man* *The Wooden Star* *The Seven Sexes*

And more—more authors—more titles
more coming!

Send for our complete catalog and instructions for ordering by mail —write to Dept. CS, Ballantine Books, Inc. 36 West 20th Street, New York 10003, N.Y.

The great masterpieces of fantasy by
J. R. R. TOLKIEN
The Hobbit

and

The Lord of the Rings

Part I—THE FELLOWSHIP OF THE RING

Part II—THE TWO TOWERS

Part III—THE RETURN OF THE KING

plus
The Tolkien Reader

Smith of Wootton Major and Farmer Giles of Ham

The Road Goes Ever On: A Song Cycle
(music by Donald Swann)

Note: These are the complete and authorized paper-bound editions, published only by Ballantine Books.

To order by mail, send $1.00 for each book (except for *The Road Goes Ever On* which requires $3.00) to Dept. CS, Ballantine Books, 36 West 20th Street, New York, N. Y. 10003.

The Exciting World of Gor

John Norman has created a series that we predict will be as famous as Burroughs' marvelous Martian books. Here is the creation of a whole new world, strange creatures, weird growths, ingenious devices coupled with breathtaking action in a totally new culture.

Don't Miss Any of the Series

TARNSMAN OF GOR

OUTLAW OF GOR

PRIEST-KINGS OF GOR

NOMADS OF GOR
